Endors

I like the way you have brought practical points out from the Bible stories you share in various chapters and how you have applied these things to everyday life. You do a good job of telling the Bible stories in an engaging way. I commend you on the work you have put into this effort! God bless!

—Rev. Rick McGough,
Local Church Apologetics

—⟋⟍—

Mary takes us through a journey of Bible characters along with unabashed insight into her own life as she teaches us God's word and lessons that she has learned. I know you will be blessed.

—Darlene Hunter Smith

—⟋⟍—

Extremely well written. The dialog is very good. Your imagination of the era is very compelling and pure. I learned about the details of David's life. I loved the "Carry On" poem. Being broken is not a failure. Also, Great ending! Truly excellent! This author has made footprints in the world and has something to say.

—Jeff Stoecker

—⟋⟍—

I loved Mary Stegmiller's open and candid thoughts, ideas, and experiences that were aptly applied to her book's theme. It is well worth a read!

—Micky Ivers

Crissy,

LIFE LESSONS
FROM KING DAVID
AND GRANDMA

Meeting + getting to
know you a little
in this last year
has been great.

You are an
inspiration to me.

Mary

LIFE LESSONS FROM KING DAVID AND GRANDMA

Discover New Life in Ancient Stories, Find Your Courage, and Learn to *"Carry On"*

MARY M. STEGMILLER

Alive with the Bible Series, Book I

Published by Author Academy Elite
P.O. Box 43, Powell, OH 43035
www.AuthorAcademyElite.com

Identifiers:
LCCN: **2019912499**
ISBN: 978-1-64085-862-6
ISBN: 978-1-64085-863-3
ISBN-978-1-64085-864-0

Available in paperback, hardback, and e-book.

Scripture quotations are taken from the New American Standard Bible, NASB copyright, 1960, 1962, 1963, 1968, 1971, 1972, 1973, 1975, 1977, 1995 by the Lockman Foundation. Used by permission.

Any Internet addresses (websites, blogs, etc.) printed in this book are offered as a resource. They are not intended in any way to be or imply an endorsement by Author Academy Elite., nor does Author Academy Elite vouch for the content of these sites and numbers for the life of this book.

Interior design by: Jetlaunch

Cover design by: Infinite Design in 99designs

Logo designs by: J.J. Stoecker

For the word of God is living and active and sharper than any two-edged sword, and piercing as far as the division of soul and spirit, of both joints and marrow, and able to judge the thoughts and intentions of the heart.
                                        —Hebrews 10:12

CONTENTS

Part III: Relationships with Others

Appendices

PREFACE

This is a story of love, life, and learning. It tells how David became a man after God's own heart. The story will share the lessons David learned and what I, Grandma, learned from it. The chapters follow three stages in David's growth and development: having a good self-image, growing a heart for God, and developing a heart for people.

It's a story of how God chose a shepherd boy and made him a king. This first book begins with David's birth and ends with him at thirty-six. David's story is very long. My second book continues his life story as king. Book II will explain the "Seventy Years Later" story, included at the beginning of this book. For the reader's guidance and inspiration, I have added lessons that I learned and my poetry. I wrote this story asking for wisdom from God.

The Bible Is Difficult

The problem is three-fold:

1. People are not relating to the Bible because they are looking at the ancient environment, which is different from their own.

2. People do not relate to the Bible characters because of the time difference.

3. When people don't relate to the Bible, they don't read it; however, God's word transcends the time difference. It has wisdom for today, and people are missing it.

I Write to Make the Bible Come Alive

The God of the Bronze age is the same God of the electric age. His messages and stories have meaning that transcends the ages. The struggles and lessons King David learned are the same things we struggle with today—good and evil. Daily we choose, the same as David—sometimes rightly and sometimes wrongly. None of it is a surprise to God, yet He loves us.

The conversations and feelings are fictional, unless quoted as actual scripture. This is a biblical fiction story.

When I read the Bible, these stories zoom around in my head. I hope you enjoy them and find them to be useful applications for your life.

In this book, I might take what others see as a most obscure Bible text and weave it into a human story. I add feelings and words to Bible characters. This is not only for entertainment but to make the Bible come alive for the reader.

I have added my personal stories, poems, and observations—to share what I have learned from studying scripture and talking and praying to God. I write about my life-learned lessons to help the reader connect with the Bible and God.

At one time, I felt depressed and unloved; I was not listening to God's voice. I could not complete this book. Since then, I learned, or remembered, that God does love me, and I stopped self-sabotaging my own life.

If you have ever felt far away from God or useless in any way, I write to show how God cares for you and has a purpose for you.

I did not want to share my life, but my cousin Mickey, first, and then others, said that my personal experiences would make this book more meaningful.

So, although I wanted to stay the unknown author, I am now adding my personal experiences, insights, and poetry because the Bible is alive to me.

So, I write to make the Bible come alive for you!

I'm Not Wise

I'm not wise on my own,
And I do not understand.
I cannot hear Your voice,
Or obey your every command.

Your words in my Bible
Are most dear to me.
But lacking in discernment—
They're confusing unto me.

If my life is an example,
Then look at my mistakes.
When placed at a crossroad,
I don't know which way to take.

I'm so easily tricked—
By things that seem all right,
But lacking in discernment,
I can't discern what's right.

Love and compassion are
The gifts You gave to me,
For them I am most blessed,
And I give my thanks to Thee.

Now to my dear God,
Who gives most generously,
I ask for wisdom and discernment—
To use my gifts for Thee.

ACKNOWLEDGEMENTS

The opinions expressed within this book are based upon the author's personal opinions and faith. Evidence supporting the author's opinion may not be inclusive of all sides, so it is at the reader's sole discretion to research these issues further if they want to learn more.

FOR INSPIRATION

First, to God who deserves all the glory for any inspiration I have received!

To Kary Oberbrunner, for creating the Author Academy Elite and the Igniting Souls tribe. You have changed my life and ignited it.

To Dick Loehr for sage advice— "Tell the truth, work hard, and carry on."

ENCOURAGEMENT AND HELP

To my cousins, Mickey and Darlene: you kept me encouraged and on track.

To Jeff, who has helped with graphics and story development.

To my husband, Kenny, who allowed me the time and finances to invest in myself and write this book.

To all my Igniting Soul friends who also have encouraged me and taught me how to write a book. It was hard work, and you helped me all along the way. I made many mistakes. I had multiple questions. I appreciate your support, your guidance, and your patience.

To all my friends who helped me promote my book and set speaking engagements—you made it all worthwhile.

INTRODUCTION

I begin with a short passage from the end of King David's life. Afterall, the end one's life portrays how well a life was lived, and what was important. In this passage:

- Who is spying on him and why?

- Who is he looking to kiss?

- What is significant about *always*?

The answers are in the books that follow. Stay tuned...

—ɯ—

This is the first book of a series. It will take David from his birth to his thirties, when he is crowned as king of Judah at Hebron. It will include family history and his heart for God. The story relates how God chooses David to be the next king, the battle with Goliath, and David's relationship with Saul, Jonathan, and Bathsheba.

—⸱⸱⸱—

Most of his forty-year reign is covered in book II of this series. The second book will include David's children and wives. It will also follow his conquering Jerusalem and his enemies. Although David sins, God never leaves David, but God does correct him. David will live to be seventy. His reign as king is seven and a half years at Hebron and thirty-three years in Jerusalem.

PROLOGUE

Seventy Years after David's Birth

"I don't know what King David is saying. He barely whispers," says the maiden. She is a beautiful young woman sent to comfort the king.

The large chief servant snaps, "Well, find out! That's why I picked you! Surely heads will roll when this is all through, and we had better be on the side that keeps theirs. Do you understand? Hmm …" He growls as he leans down to look at the maiden, who only comes up to his chest.

He looks deep into her eyes.

"Yyyyes," she stutters and whimpers. She hangs her head and covers her eyes. The tears are flowing now. The fear for herself and her family has paralyzed her. She can't think.

Seeing that her fear simply makes her collapse, he softens his response, saying, "I know you are doing your best; I am sorry I scared you."

He slowly turns her toward him. With his fingertips, he gently lifts her head up to make her look back into his eyes. He offers a fake smile.

He softly repeats, "I am sorry if I scared you. I picked you because I trust you. Now tell me what his mumbling sounds like. Are there any words or sounds that repeat? Let me figure it out! Now close your eyes and play it back in your mind. Tell me what you heard."

She closes her eyes and recalls the past. "At first, he didn't speak to me. The guards would escort me out anytime he had a visitor. So, I don't know who was seeing him, or what he said to them."

He lets go of her chin. He growls again and looks away.

She knows her family will be richly rewarded, as promised, if she can deliver some good information. She pushes herself to recall something.

"Uh ... but in his sleep, he says things. Since he is becoming weaker and his vision is fading sometimes, he thinks I am someone else. Then he has mumbled and talked to me. There are repeats like, uh, he says 'num' and 'one.' Then, let's see, there's a 'love you,' and I think it's an ... an 'always.' And sometimes, he has the start of a smile when he whispers 'always,' and then he has squeezed my hand. He seems happy then. Other times, he just thrashes, and shouts, 'No!'"

She shakes again, afraid her knowledge is too limited, and she starts to cry, "That's all I can remember!" She is sobbing now.

The chief servant knows she is only allowed a short respite, and soon others will wonder why he is holding her up. Her words mean more to him than to her. He pats her shoulder and adds, "Finish eating. You need to go back—and stop crying before the guards ask you why. You have done well."

He sends her on her way—back to the king. Immediately, he sends a cryptic message to Adonijah. "Need to act soon before another is chosen."

Since then, several weeks pass, and so much happens since that conversation. It makes her head spin; the events are very confusing. Yet, she remains oblivious to her part. Today, after her brief minutes of repose, she returns to comfort the king. She dreads touching him. He is so cold; he can't stay warm. He senses her approaching and reaches for her hand. He can no longer see. She reaches out to him. He takes her hand, kisses it with his dry lips, and whispers, "Always," as King David passes from this life.

PART I
IDENTITY—
SELF-ESTEEM

1
THE MAKING OF A KING; BEGIN AT THE BOTTOM

KING DAVID IS a king, leader, ruler, judge, enforcer, warrior, and military champion. He is honored and is still loved centuries after his death. He must have been a delight and loved by everyone all his life. He must have been born with skills to be a successful leader. He must have come from a great, wealthy, and important family. He must have been honored and highly respected by his own family.

No, not even a little bit.

Not so, not by the Bible—and not the way I see it. Let me tell you why.

David is born the eighth son of Jesse. He also has two older half-sisters. He is ruddy, maybe red-headed. Family history shows that his father could have been considered a half-breed, or at least not a full-blooded Hebrew. His grandmother, Ruth, came from the foreign country of Moab. His great-great-grandmother, Rahab, was a prostitute from Jericho.

Jesse loves his grandmother, Ruth. He is prepared to be buried next to her, but that doesn't mean people don't talk about Ruth being a Moabite. Is the ruddiness from that line? Will people talk again and make fun of Jesse's family?

David's hometown is Bethlehem, a small hilly village, not a big city. Bethlehem means house of bread. Its first name was Ephrata, or Ephrathah, meaning fruitfulness. Sometimes in scripture, both names are used. Yes, David was from a farming community—not a place you would expect to find the next king.

But God doesn't look at things the way we do. Foreseeing the future king, Jesus, will come from David's line, God inspired the prophet Micah to write.

> But as for you, Bethlehem Ephrathah, too little to be among the clans of Judah, from you One will go forth for Me to be ruler in Israel. His goings forth are from long ago, from the days of eternity.
>
> —Micah 5:2

David is from Bethlehem Ephrathah. It is about a half mile above sea level and surrounded by other hills. The hills are full of caves, boulders and rocks. There is a legend that God had sent an angel carrying a huge sack of rocks for the earth. The sack broke over Israel, scattering the rocks everywhere.

Even today, you can see an abundance of rocks and boulders throughout the land. David would have had to learn how to lead his sheep throughout this rough terrain.

Before he becomes a leader of people, he was a leader of sheep. And for the task of shepherding, he had to be taught. Shepherd training would have started from his family—possibly with one of his older brothers.

—⁕—

Eliab is the oldest, and he objects. "Don't think that I am going to be the one to train David. I'm not spending my days with him. He's a little runt and Mommy's favorite. And besides being a spoiled brat, he's weak and obnoxious. It's not happening with me; just get that into your head. I'm not going with him." He points his finger at Abinadab, the second oldest son.

"Hey, I totally agree. I think the little runt should go to Shammah," Abinadab answers.

They nod, laugh, and call to the third oldest son, "Shammah, got a job for you."

—⁓—

The family is large, and Eliab and Abinadab know they won't be without tasks. They are looking forward to being soldiers for Saul, and they agree to work the fields.

When their daily chores are done, they enjoy working on their fighting skills. It will be even more fun to entreat their nephews to join in the play.

Sticks can be used for sword fighting, and there is always time for wrestling.

—⁓—

Eliab says, "Yeah, I'd rather watch Abishai, Joab, and Asahel go at it than watch sheep. Let's teach them to throw a spear and sword fight. You take Abishai, and I'll take Joab. That Joab is strong! He's younger but he has a killer instinct, and he hates to lose. Then we'll let Asahel challenge the winner."

Abinadab replies, "Sounds like fun. I'm game, and they will love it too. Just hold Joab back a little. Sometimes he fights dangerously or mean, especially if he's losing; then he'll aim for fingers or eyes. We can't let him permanently injure his brothers."

Eliab laughs. "All right, I'll see if I can rein him in some and teach him to fight fair. Just think, someday they might fight at our side in a real battle. We'll ask to have them work in the fields so we will be done at the same time."

—✺—

Shammah is the third oldest. He also plans to become a soldier. However, he does have a little more diplomacy than his older brothers. Names are important and are often changed as a character or circumstance dictates a change. Shammah, his name now means desolation. But later in life, he is known as Shimeah, which means fame. Maybe he was born in or after a storm, a drought, or death in the family, and desolation was on his parents' minds.

Shammah's two older brothers are his father's favorites—especially Eliab. They all know the oldest will inherit a double portion and is expected to be a leader in the family. Shammah also has five younger brothers and two older sisters. He has learned to negotiate, as well as appreciate, the strengths and weaknesses of his siblings and nephews. He sees value in his family and David.

David is clever and observant, which seems to irritate Eliab. David, who is too young for diplomacy, shouts it out if he sees something Eliab has missed. Shammah laughs as he recalls David shouting at Eliab, "Eliab, the sheep need more water!" … or … "Eliab, the latch needs to be fixed on the gate, or the sheep will get out!"

There were several other incidents. Shammah can picture his mother snickering. No wonder Eliab thinks David is his mother's favorite.

Yes, David probably is his mother's favorite. He recalls his mom humming and singing to David as she had done for all of them. It is one of his favorite memories of her.

—⚬⚬—

Sleep Baby

Peace to you, my little one,
Close those big brown eyes now.
David's tired; time for sleep.
Time for little ones to sleep.

Go to sleep, and say goodnight
For tomorrow'll be bright.
Go to sleep and say goodnight
For tomorrow'll be bright.

—⚬⚬—

Shammah smiles as he remembers how his mother changed the song to match each child. She was so clever.

He hums, "Shammah's tired … hmm." Yep, he can remember the song being sung to him.

Shammah sees his mother worried about David surviving. He remembers that his father, Jesse, didn't think David would live. Shammah recalls the look on his father's face and how he paced around after David was born. He heard Eliab ask Jesse about the baby.

He remembers how Jesse shook his head and muttered, "It's a boy," and then added, "but I don't think he'll make it."

Also worried, his mother puts more love into David. She never ceases to pray for her eighth son—the very last of her children. He is a ruddy baby, which has caused his father to scoff at his complexion. She heard Jesse call him *the runt;* that hurt her more than all her labor pains.

She holds David close and prays over him again and again, "God, please bless my David, be close to him, help him become the man you desire of him. Please bless him always."

She sings softly to the baby. He smiles in his sleep as she holds him in her arms. She feels it in her heart that God is answering this prayer.

She imagines that God is saying, "Yes, I will bless him, and he will not be the least of your sons."

She looks to heaven and wonders if she is having a delusion or if God is answering her prayer. She has no idea that David will become the ruler of all Israel. Nonetheless, she continues to pray for David. Even if the answer she imagines wasn't God's answer, she believes, hopes, and prays for good things for her baby. She holds him close, rocks him, and softly sings.

—⁓—

Little Baby Red

Oh, little baby,
All ruddy and red,
Papa thinks you are
Something to dread.

Mama loves her baby,
My little baby red.
Mama prays God's blessings,
His blessings instead.

—⁓—

The baby coos as she sings. She believes he likes her singing to him. She muses, *Maybe he will sing for the king someday.*

Shammah replays in his head this history of David, his father's comments, and his mother's singing. Shammah thinks of his own birth name. *They named me Shammah (desolation). I bet they didn't think I'd make it, either. That's something David and I have in common. But we did make it. We survived. And David has fight in him too! Besides that, he is family, and family is important.*

Shammah muses, *And besides, I might as well make the best of it. Eliab is going to make me do it anyway. I will teach David how to survive. I will teach him how to protect his sheep and himself. And God willing*—Shammah looks to heaven—*God Himself will watch over David when I am not there.*

Shammah takes David with him to begin the shepherding lessons.

—m—

David is aware Eliab has chosen to be with the nephews—Abishai, Joab, and Asahel—and he questions Shammah.

"Why doesn't Eliab like me?"

Shammah thinks before responding. "Well, Eliab and Abinadab want to be soldiers. Eliab thinks you are Mom's favorite. You know how he fawns over Joab and admires his strength. He thinks you're weak and will be eaten by wolves, and he doesn't want to be responsible for that ... or to get close to you, as you might be gone soon enough." He smiles.

David blinks in astonishment and doesn't say anything.

Shammah continues, laughs, and ruffles David's curly hair. "I'm teasing. Well, I don't feel that way, David. I am glad to teach you. I think you're smart, and I think you will do well out here. All day I have watched sheep, and they are stupid. They don't talk, and they get into trouble and lose their way. If they get hurt, then I must carry them. How could I not care more for you, my brother, and my family? And as far as surviving out here, it's not what's here ..." He points to his arms. "... it's what's here." He points to his head and his heart. "I think you will do fine. What do you think?"

David kicks the dust in the trail as they walk along. The sheep are following behind them. "Well, he's right. I'm not as strong as Abishai or Joab, and I'm not fast like Asahel. But you're right, I can learn if you show me," he says with sudden resolve.

Then David turns and looks at the herd following them and adds, "Yes, teach me, and God will help me so that I can, and I will do it. I will learn to protect myself and them."

Shammah thinks about how he had to compete with his older and bigger brothers, and he adds, "And don't worry about fighting with our nephews. I know a thing or two about fighting bigger people. I can show you a trick or two in wrestling. I'll teach you how to use that sling to throw rocks too. There's many ways to defend yourself."

They walk for a while; then Shammah adds his last bit of encouragement. "And don't forget: you do some things better than our nephews."

David thinks about it. "What's that?"

Shammah grins. "Well, none of them can carry a tune, whether singing or playing on their flutes. I'm sure the sheep will be glad not to hear their squeaking."

David smiles and touches his flute at his side. "I like playing my flute for the sheep. And I'll sing to them too. I enjoy being with the sheep. I know they're not smart; someone needs to watch over them. I don't think Eliab likes them, although he's never lost any; he always calls them stupid."

—∿—

Shammah explains to David how important it is to recognize his sheep. A good shepherd will know his sheep so well that if they get mixed with another herd, he will be able to separate them, even in the dark.

He then has David observe the sheep's predispositions. Shammah has them walking in single file between the fields. He tells David to hold the staff across the path, so the lead sheep must jump over it. Then he's to move the staff out of the way before the following sheep get there.

David laughs as he sees all the following sheep jump at that point, even though there is no longer anything to jump over.

Shammah says, "See how important it is to lead? The sheep follow the leader without thinking about it. They jump there because the one in front of them jumped at that place. You will be their leader; be a good one."

David vows he will.

—∿—

We know David succeeds and is a shepherd for several years. Shammah goes on to be a soldier, and David has care of the flock of sheep by himself.

During his years of shepherding, David protects the sheep from both a lion and a bear.

The mundane tasks of shepherding help David learn:

1. How to recognize his sheep

2. How to protect himself and them

3. How to throw rocks with a sling

4. How to survive and hide in the land

The physical labor helps him grow stronger.

A good shepherd would use the rocks along the hillsides to make a corral. At night, he would lie down across the opening. Any predator would have to get by him to grab a sheep.

David writes in his Psalms:

> I am the good shepherd; the good shepherd lays down His life for the sheep.
> —John 10:11

David draws closer to God. He understands that although he is the shepherd to the sheep, God is his shepherd.

> 1 The Lord is my shepherd; I shall not want.
> 2 He makes me to lie down in green pastures;
> He leads me beside quiet waters.
> —Psalm 23:1-2

David knows the sheep fear the loud noise of a river splashing. Still water, or quiet water, is the water they want. God helps him find still water for himself and his sheep.

13 For You formed my inward parts;
You wove me in my mother's womb.
14 I will give thanks to You,
For I am fearfully and wonderfully made.
                                        —Psalm 139:13,14

David sees himself fearfully and wonderfully made by God.

—m—

When I doubted my own self-worth, I had trouble writing or speaking to people. I was so busy criticizing myself that I could not handle outside criticism. Even constructive criticism would shut me down. I feared what people would say or think.

I would make jokes because I was afraid of being serious.

Unlike David, when I was growing up, I had only one brother. My older brother was red-headed, and I deemed him full of fire, trickery, and trouble. When I look back, he always could convince me to do things—sometimes for good but mostly for trickery. I guess I always wanted his approval, so I would fall for the trickery. But one thing that stuck out in my mind was that he and my cousins all called me fat. And compared to all of them, I was fat.

Sixty-eight years later, I was asked to write on a sheet of paper all the negative names I called myself or other people called me. The list started off with fat. Then I filled up the sheet with a multitude of other names: divorced, messy, unorganized, failure, dropout, daydreamer, lazy, poor excuse for a mother, poor grandmother, lousy wife, and poor witness for God. I could see myself as bad at everything.

All the names I called myself were negative. I was trying to finish this Bible story that I had started years ago. Somewhere deep inside, I felt I should finish this story before I died, and at sixty-eight, how long did I have?

In preparing my writing, I was asked to do a short video—one video titled, "I Am an Author."

I was stuck. I did not have enough confidence to say that.

Eventually, I tried to do a silhouette in the video to hide my face. I mumbled something about being a dreamer and a storyteller. I said I didn't care if anyone liked my story; I was writing for God. It was a miserable fifty seconds. It came out all black with no silhouette. I didn't even want to watch it.

Then I received a gift from Kary Oberbrunner— the book Your Secret Name. I read the book and decided to take the course.

That course changed my life.

The negative names I wrote on that page are not the names God calls me. I can't even remember all the negative things I called myself. I repented of calling myself those names. And I understood I had felt unloved because I didn't love myself.

There were plenty of people who loved me, but I focused on the negative and felt unloved. I focused on all my failures.

I was married at seventeen, a mother by eighteen, and divorced at nineteen. I remarried at twenty-one, became a mother to a second child at twenty-three, then divorced again at thirty. I felt these events were failures that defined me.

I remarried for a third time at thirty-six and had two more children. Although my third husband

and I have stayed married, my feelings of failure remained with me for all those years.

At the age of sixty-eight, I could not look straight into a camera and say, "I have something to share with you; I am an author."

After learning to value God's love and appreciation for me, I can now think and act with confidence. I buried the negative names, and I repent of them. I am loved by God, and that is good enough for me.

When I learned to look at myself through God's eyes, I found the courage to carry on.

I am an author; this is my story.

The Name Game

Many are the names we're called,
Some pretty,
Some petty,
Some are downright mean.

Friend and foe, they give us names,
Trying to describe our lives.
Cast off those useless names,
And purge them from our being.

For Abba God knows us more than they,
He has, for us, a beautiful name—
A name of hope, truth and promise,
And guidance along the way.

Seek now the name that God gave you
Free yourself from those who are mean,
Find fulfilling joy in your life,
And a purpose for you to gain.

Study questions:

Who are you listening to?

How do the names you call yourself affect you?

Are negative names keeping you from accomplishing something?

How can we find God's name for us?

How can we find meaning in everyday tasks?

David didn't listen to the negative names; he listened to God.

2
SKELETONS IN YOUR CLOSET—LET THEM OUT! GOD RECOGNIZES THE FAITHFUL!

WHY DOES JESSE think this son, David, is the least of all his sons?

Maybe it is David's red complexion; maybe it is because he is the last child. Or maybe the pregnancy and delivery was hard on David's mother. Maybe it was David's birth size. We can only guess.

But we do know Jesse is asked to bring all his sons to Samuel. He brings them all except David. Only when Samuel asks if Jesse has any more sons does he admit there is David.

Probably in fear of Samuel, Jesse explains that David is the least and is away from home tending sheep. In other words, David is not worthy to be blessed by Samuel or attend the sacrifice. David is overlooked by his own father.

David doesn't feel demeaned. In his Psalm, he feels uplifted by God.

> But You, O Lord, are a shield about me, My glory, and the One who lifts my head.
> —Psalm 3:3

Despite the skepticism of his father and brothers, David looks to God for affirmation and acceptance. God can do more with David because he keeps a good self-image. He looks to God for affirmation—not the world.

Why can't Jesse see what God sees in David? Why would a father doubt his own son's worthiness? Maybe Jesse has his own issues, and David reminds him of some of these issues.

People are ... well, people. Even thousands of years ago, people were exactly as they are now. That is, people were and are made up with some goodness and some evilness in them.

People choose each word and each action in responding to others each day. If they think kindly of others, they may choose to be encouraging, helpful, good-hearted, or the like.

However, if they are thinking of elevating or defending themselves, people sometimes choose evil to protect their ego or further their own desires.

At least, their actions show that they choose evil. They attack anyone who is different. They do this by criticizing, ostracizing, lying, gossiping, stealing, snubbing, or ridiculing others.

And for those seeking power or feeding their pride, the intensity can become so great that viciousness, and even murder, is not off the table.

David knows. He knows firsthand. He knows his brothers make fun of him. His father also has issues with him. Could it be David's appearance that reminds Jesse of taunts and sneers he received as a child?

One of David's ancestors is a Moabite—Jesse's grandmother, Ruth.

And even farther back in their family history is Rahab, who was a harlot from Jericho.

Two of his forefathers married women who were not from the line of Israel. Those who are always looking to put others down like to remember that this is part of Jesse's family history.

One grandmother, Rahab, was not Hebrew, and she was a harlot. That is easy to criticize if you are a full Hebrew and you look down on harlots.

Does criticism like this make Jesse self-conscious? If David looks different from the other children, would it embarrass Jesse? Could that be why Jesse does not present David to Samuel?

God doesn't see something wrong with Rahab or David; he sees something special in them.

—〰—

Yes, Rahab lived as a harlot in Jericho. Why, we don't know. What we do know is that she had faith in the one true God. And although people look down on her, God lifts her up more than once in Bible verses.

Over a thousand years later, God inspires Paul to record this passage in Hebrews, Chapter 11—the chapter on faith:

> Now faith is the assurance of things hoped for, the conviction of things not seen.
>
> —Hebrews 11:1

We know that Rahab has faith in God before she sees the spies who enter her city of Jericho.

> By Faith the harlot Rahab did not perish along with those who were disobedient, after she welcomed the spies in peace.
>
> —Hebrews 11:31

The Israelites have been wandering in the wilderness for forty years. God provides for them. Their clothing has not even worn out. They dress as they did when they were back in Egypt. They now begin to enter into the Holy Land. They cross the Jordan and scout out the land. Two spies are sent to Jericho.

The spies try to disguise themselves; however, something gives them away. Not long after they enter Jericho, the city officials look for them. Jericho is a walled city, with walls so big that homes are built into them. The only entry is a large double gate, manned and locked at night.

—⁓—

The spies are not named in the Bible, but one is most likely Salmon.

Rahab sees them and recognizes that they are Israelite spies. Fearing God, she whispers to them, "Come in quickly; I see who you are. So do others, and soon, trouble will be upon you."

Salmon softly says, "Why should we trust you?"

She smiles and demurely points to her door but whispers softly, "They're watching. I believe in your God." And a little louder, she says, "Come in," and softer again adds, "I will explain inside."

Inside, she exclaims as she waves at her ladder to the roof, "Hurry to the roof, I will hide you Israelites there."

Salmon asks, "Why do you think we are Israelites?"

She flaps her hands with nervousness, and gently prods them forward toward the ladder. "Your sandals show with each step! They aren't like anything our men wear. I saw, and so did that young man;

he's running to tell the king. But first, he listened to see what I said to you."

Nervously, she adds, "May your God have mercy on me for helping you, and may He protect us."

8 Now before they lay down, she came to them on the roof,
9 and said to the men, "I know that the Lord has given you the land, and the terror of you has fallen on us, and that all the inhabitants of the land have melted away before you.
10 For we have heard how the Lord dried up the water of the Red Sea before you when you came out of Egypt, and what you did to the two kings of the Amorites who were beyond the Jordan, to Sihon and Og, whom you utterly destroyed.
11 When we heard it, our hearts melted and no courage remained in any man any longer because of you; for the Lord your God He is God in heaven above and on earth beneath. Now therefore, please swear to me by the Lord, since I have dealt kindly with you, that you also will deal kindly with my father's household, and give me a pledge of truth,
13 and spare my father and my mother and my brothers and my sisters with all who belong to them and deliver our lives from death.
—Joshua 2:8-13

Salmon answers, "Our God is a jealous God; He will have no other gods before Him. We cannot bring you and your gods, your idols, your religion, or your family of idol worshipers into our camp."

Wringing her hands with tears in her eyes, she answers, "These people have enslaved me and my family. Neither they nor their gods have helped us in our misery. We were so hungry, and none of them would trade with us, give us food, or help us. I was marked for this ..." She points to her harlot garb. "... this or to be sacrificed alive. My whole family was banned until I agreed.

"I heard how your God sent food from heaven to earth for your people, and that they are many thousands and thousands. Your God is a God of heaven and earth, as I said, and a God of love.

"My family and I will serve him. We do not worship the false gods since we saw they did not care for us. We have faith only in your God. I swear this is the belief of all my family. Please, teach us how to worship your God, and save us from this evil town."

Upon hearing this, both men agree to help her.

She thinks a minute, then asks, "Do you have permission to speak for your people? Will your king agree?" She bites her lip and waits for their response.

Salmon's friend answers, "We are from the tribe of Judah. We have no king. Joshua leads us. But with you is one of the Lions of Judah." He points to Salmon.

Salmon looks deeply at her and sees her eyes are tearing now, and when she stops biting her lip, it begins to quiver. He can see how she has been tormented with lies and unfulfilled promises. It touches him deeply; it brings out a new feeling. He wants to protect her from all the mean and hurtful people who ever lied to her.

He clears his throat. "He is teasing me. I am from the tribe of Judah, and a lion is our symbol. My father, Nahshon, is the leader of our tribe. And yes, my word will carry your protection and your family's. I promise it."

"Here, Rahab, have this token of my promise." He removes the leather strap around his neck with a token he made for himself. It is engraved with a symbol of a lion. He sets it on her table. "When we come to conquer this city, you and your family must stay here in your home. Do not leave. When it is all finished, show this token and ask for Salmon. I will protect you."

Relieved, she replies, "Good! I have a plan not just to hide you but also for your escape. Hide here now and be quiet."

Then she hides them on her roof and covers them with flax.

It does not take long for the news to reach the king. He immediately sends his men to find the spies. The king's men come to her home and question her. One of them demands, "Where are the two spies that were seen entering here?"

Rahab answers, feigning a shocked look, "What? Spies in my house? Well, there were two men here, but they didn't stay. They had nothing to trade, so I sent them away. And after they left, I watched them until I saw them leave through the gate. If you hurry, you can catch them."

The soldiers search her house quickly, and finding no spies, leave at once in hot pursuit. The leader orders the gate shut and locked behind them. Jericho is a walled city, and the only way in or out is the gate.

It appears that the spies have no escape and are trapped in Jericho. However, Rahab has more plans.

God only knows where Rahab had found enough red twine to make a long rope. This is not what ropes are usually made of; it must have been made in secret. However, she finds it, and for a long time, weaves it into this rope. Had she made this rope for her escape and her family?

As we know, Jericho's walls are thick enough for homes to be built into them, and Rahab's home is one of these. She has a window that is built into the wall. It is too far to the ground to jump from the widow, but with the rope, the spies can climb down and get outside of the wall.

When it is dark, she brings the spies down from the roof into her home and shows them the rope.

She teases, "Well, can a lion climb down a rope?"

Salmon smiles. "I am a man. And yes, I can. We offered you protection, and here's what you are to do. This rope will mark you. When we come to attack, you are to hang it outside your window. Also, any of your family you wish to rescue must be in here with you. If any of you go outside, it is to your own peril."

She agrees to his plan. Then she tells them to hide in the hills and not return to their camp for three days. She knows the soldiers sent to seek them will give up after three days. She silently prays to their God to protect them. She also prays that God will help her and her family escape Jericho.

—⁓—

God remembers Rahab as faithful. I am sure some people remember her as a foreigner and a harlot, but it is God's view that counts.

Rahab marries Salmon and is David's great-great-grandmother. People might have criticized Salmon and their son Boaz. Is it possible that criticism goes even further down the family line? Was Jesse criticized because Boaz is his grandfather?

The family could choose to remember how Rahab's faith in God saved her or choose to remember that she was a harlot, born in Jericho. Mean people would point out that she was not a daughter of Jacob, and that she had been a harlot.

Her family could choose to let words sting, from listening to mean and negative people, or they could choose to look through God's eyes and admire her faith in God. They could appreciate how God honored her faith by saving her and her family. Each family member could choose either to be embarrassed or to be proud of Rahab. Everyone got to choose their own point of view. I wonder which one Jesse chose.

—ᴍ—

God said in the Bible that Rahab had faith.

And without faith it is impossible to please Him, for he who comes to God must believe that He is a rewarder of those who seek Him.
—Hebrews 11:6

30 By faith the walls of Jericho fell down after they had been encircled for seven days.
31 By faith Rahab the harlot did not perish along with those who were disobedient, after she welcomed the spies in peace.
—Hebrews 11:30-31

David has faith in God also. He writes this in one of his Psalms to God.

4 How blessed is the man who has made the Lord his trust, and has not turned to the proud, nor to those who lapse into falsehood.

5 Many, O Lord my God, are the wonders which You have done, And Your thoughts toward us; There is none to compare with You. If I would declare and speak of them, they would be too numerous to count.

—Psalm 40:4-5

—◦◦—

At times, my own faith was smaller than a mustard seed. More than once, I felt like committing suicide. I was so disappointed with life and myself; I did not want to go on.

In grade school (which went up to eighth grade), one of the questions on standardized tests was, "What do you want to be when you grow up?"

We were to write in the answer, but I never knew what to write. Every year, I wrote something different. I was told the teachers liked teacher for an answer. Other classmates suggested that doctor or lawyer were good answers too. What I really wanted was to be married and to have children.

One of my high school teachers said we should set goals for ourselves. My goal was to be at least eighteen before I had my first child. (And I made it!)

I'm sure he would have suggested having children at an older age or to graduate from college first. But he didn't ask us to tell him our goals.

My first husband pursued me like a stalker. I didn't know what that was, or that stalker behavior was abnormal. I thought it was love. Apparently, it was manipulation. He was pursuing others and was sexually active with them when not around me.

Also, the Vietnam conflict was at its height in 1967-8. He was going into the army. He pointed out that he could die. He wanted to get married.

He was one of four young men who were going into the army at that time. They signed up as buddies—two sets of two. Somehow, my husband got released during his advanced training. The other three went to Vietnam. One of them, a handsome young man named Jerry, came home in a casket. Sometimes, eighteen is all the older you get.

I had also buried a classmate who had died in a car accident before our junior year. I guess it left me with the feeling that life is fleeting, and I'd better get at it.

I never thought I would live to be as old as I am.

Anyway, I wanted to be married and loved, whether it was God's choice for me or not. In fact, I felt it was not God's choice. I remember trying to tell God that he was wrong—this would all work out for good. I knew my boyfriend had lied to me. I was sure I could change him; however, I could not change him. Our son was born the next year, and that did not change him, either.

The emotional cracks in my personality were on the way.

I thought I would be married forever, so when I filed for divorce at nineteen ... crack. Also, I was afraid of him. He could become violent ... crack.

There were all the negative names he called me ... crack. All the mistakes I made that he pointed out ... crack. Nineteen, a mom, divorced, high school dropout ... crack.

I had done it my way, not God's way.

I did not like myself or where I was in life, but I had my son. I had to carry on.

Study Questions

Is faith in God part of the legacy that Rahab and Salmon left to their family?

What is the legacy that you are leaving for your family?

What can you do to show faith?

How can you encourage your family to have their faith in God?

We need to rename our skeletons. Rahab could have been called the harlot or the faithful. What do you call her?

What do you call yourself?

How can you look for the good in yourself and others and see as God sees?

3
MORE SKELETONS? AND MORE FOREIGNERS TOO? GOD ADMIRES LOYALTY!

WHAT DOES RUDDINESS mean to David and his family? Does it mean David could be a redhead? If David is redheaded, why is that a problem? Wasn't Moses redheaded? And Moses was the one who led them out of Egypt.

How is it that David being ruddish is bothersome to Jesse?

Jesse, what's the matter with having a redheaded son?

Well, are we back to the insults? Is Jesse insulted about his family?

Esau was considered ruddy—a redhead. He fathered the Edomites, and they lived next to Moab.

They often intermarried with Moabites. They were not Israelites. The Israelites came from Esau's brother, Jacob, whom God later renamed Israel.

Jesse's grandmother, Ruth, was a Moabite. And their history has a sordid tale.

It all starts with Abraham and his nephew Lot.

—m—

Before Abraham has children, he travels with his nephew, Lot. They wander about Israel, herding animals and living in tents.

Lot has his own herds and herdsmen, and Abraham has his. There is often strife between the herdsmen, and Abraham and Lot decide to separate. Abraham lets Lot choose, and Lot chooses the lush land along the Jordan river.

Lot moves his herds there, but he grows tired of tent life. He has servants who can watch his flocks, so he chooses to move to the city of Sodom. He lives there with his wife and his two daughters.

Sodom and its sister city of Gomorrah are known for their evilness. While Lot lives there, God decides to destroy both cities. Angels come and tell Abraham of the upcoming destruction planned for Sodom and Gomorrah. Abraham barters with God to spare the cities if there are even ten righteous people. However, there are not ten righteous people to be found there. Lot, his wife, and two daughters who are engaged to be married do not total ten believers.

Then Abraham begs God to save Lot. God sends the two angels to warn Lot and his family.

The two future sons-in-law scoff at the warning of destruction. Lot is so fearful he doesn't know what to do. The angels take pity on him and lead him out of the city with his wife and daughters. The daughters' fiancées refuse to go.

Then bad goes to worse. One of the angels tells them not to look back at the destruction of the city, but Lot's wife, Ado, cannot resist. She looks back and is at once turned into a pillar of salt. Now the four survivors are only three: one father and two daughters.

Lot had originally asked the angels permission to go to the city of Zoar, but now he is afraid to stay there. Fearfully, Lot flees to the hills, taking his two daughters with him. He chooses a cave for their new home.

Lot is even afraid to return to Abraham, who had prayed for Lot's safety. So fearful is Lot now, that he wants to avoid any city life. He decides to become a hermit, planning to live in the cave with his two daughters.

The daughters fear they will live out the rest of their lives as hermits also. What will happen to them after their father dies? They feel they need sons. As time passes, they become fearful and angry, and this is what they plot.

They bring their father alcohol and encourage him to drink until he passes out. While he is out cold, they have intercourse with him, hoping to conceive. Their plan works, and two sons are born from this incestuous scheme—one to each daughter.

—〰—

What is the fear that drives the daughters to such a scheme?

In those days, women could not own property. Their worth and protection came from producing sons. Husbands were probably fifteen, maybe thirty years older or more. Their father would protect his daughters while they were young and arrange a marriage for them during their teenage years. At midlife, it was common for a woman to have buried both her first two protectors—her father and her husband. And when both the husband and father had died, she would need a new protector. Without a son, what would become of her? Since women could not own property, any property their earlier protector had owned would be turned over to the next closest male heir. That is why, for their own protection, Lot's daughters seduced him to have sons. The Moabites and the Ammonites came from these two sons of incest.

> 37 The firstborn bore a son, and called his name Moab; he is the father of the Moabites to this day. 38 As for the younger, she also bore a son, and called his name Ben-Ammi; he is the father of the sons of Ammon to this day.

—Genesis 19: 37, 38

How does this history affect David or Jesse? The Moabites live next to Edomites, the descendants of Esau, the redhead. They often intermarry.

Jesse's grandmother Ruth is a Moabite. If David is a redhead, did it come from the incestuous Moabite connection to the family?

Ruth is a foreigner, but she is also loyal. God admires her loyalty. Here is her story.

—⁂—

After years of famine in Judah, Jesse's great-grand-mother, Naomi, and her family move to Moab. The family then consists of Naomi, her husband, and their two sons.

While living in Moab, both her sons marry Moabite women. Although married, neither daughter-in-law has conceived.

We don't know why, and the Bible does not say, but her husband and then both sons die in Moab. Now Naomi has no protectors because there are no males in the family. She has only her two daughters-in-law.

Naomi lives there for ten years. She is too old to marry and conceive. She returns to Bethlehem, in Judea, to die. She says goodbye to her daughters-in-law. She tells them to return to their families and their gods. But one of her daughters-in-law, Ruth,

will not do so. She is not going back to her family.
She is going with Naomi.

> 14 And they lifted up their voices and wept again;
> and Orpah kissed her mother-in-law, but Ruth
> clung to her.
> 15 Then she said, "Behold, your sister-in-law
> has gone back to her people and her gods; return
> after your sister-in-law."
> 16 But Ruth said, "Do not urge me to leave you
> or turn back from following you; for where you
> go, I will go, and where you lodge, I will lodge.
> Your people shall be my people, and your God,
> my God.
> 17 "Where you die, I will die, and there I will be
> buried. Thus may the Lord do to me, and worse,
> if anything but death parts you and me."
> 18 When she saw that she was determined to go
> with her, she said no more to her.
> 19 So they both went until they came to
> Bethlehem. And when they had come to
> Bethlehem, all the city was stirred because of
> them, and the women said, "Is this Naomi?"
> 20 She said to them, "Do not call me Naomi;
> call me Mara, for the Almighty has dealt very
> bitterly with me.
> 21 "I went out full, but the Lord has brought
> me back empty. Why do you call me Naomi,
> since the Lord has witnessed against me and the
> Almighty has afflicted me?"
> 22 So Naomi returned, and with her Ruth the
> Moabitess, her daughter-in-law, who returned

from the land of Moab. And they came to Bethlehem at the beginning of barley harvest.
—Ruth 1:14-22

When they arrive in Bethlehem, the whole town gossips about Naomi's return. Some are glad, and some are not. Early in the day, the women share any new stories at the water hole. Not all the women are mean; there are three who are kind. One is older, and two are younger. All of them have empathy.

The first remarks, "Naomi has returned. Poor Naomi."

"Oh, what's the matter? Did her husband die? Did her sons bring her home?" the second one asks.

"They are dead—all the men, her husband, and sons all dead," the third, older lady answers.

"That is horrible! Was it an accident? What happened? Does she have grandsons?" replies the first one.

"No, no grandchildren," answers the third lady.

The second woman asks, "Oh, she is all alone, and traveled back here by herself?"

"Well, one daughter-in-law came with her, and no, she's not with child," responds the older lady.

The first sensitive lady says, "A Hebrew woman who lived in Moab? At least Naomi has that!"

"No, she's a Moabite. Ruth is her name," the older lady replies.

The first responds, "A Moabite? Didn't she have a family? Why didn't she go back to her own Moabite family?"

The older lady explains, "She's devoted to Naomi. Naomi said Ruth believes in our God, the one true God."

The first replies, "My grandma said Naomi has always been kind, so why did this happen to her?"

The elder lady says, "That is the way she feels; she feels God has dealt harshly with her. She's sad. She said we should call her Mara. It means bitterness. She doesn't want to be called Naomi anymore (*which means pleasant*). She's always been kind. We know that she must have treated Ruth well because Ruth has left her family to come here, and that had to be a hard thing to do. Naomi says that Ruth follows our ways. She is pretty and willing to work. She's not begging for handouts. She said she will work for both herself and Naomi. Even after that long trip, she's going today to glean in the fields. Here she comes to gather water."

—◊—

Just as some people look for good, some people look for bitterness and meanness, and some want to spread their bitterness. Tired of nice talk, although no one has spoken to her, one bitter woman now steps up. It is her intention to take over and turn the sentiment a different direction.

The first bitter woman says, "We should keep away; she's a curse. Look what happened to Naomi. They never should have moved to Moab. We should keep with our own people, or God will judge us too."

Other women listen and they, too, have decided they don't like this foreigner, especially a pretty one. They've been waiting for like-minded people to speak out. Up until now, they whisper to each other. Now one joins in the attack.

The second bitter woman adds, "Yeah, Naomi's back. Ha! I heard a couple of beggar women had walked into town. It was just Naomi coming back with her tail between her legs. She goes to an evil, godless country with her two sickly sons and wonders why God is not blessing her. And this daughter-in-law, she believes in our God? I don't believe that. She is not a daughter of Abraham, or Israel, or Judah. She is an incestuous offspring of Lot's brood. I'll bet there is more to her story than devotion to Naomi. What kind of family would want their daughter married to one of Naomi's sons, anyway? Neither of those boys were strong enough even to father a child. So, what is she doing here? We don't need her matching with one of our men and making half-breeds. She should go back home. I guess they accept mixed marriages there. Ha!"

Some of the young girls agree. They don't want this pretty, God-fearing foreign woman in their village. She might marry someone they have an eye on. They also fear the next attack on them, especially if they disagree. So, they whisper, and one asks, "Well, what is she doing here?"

—⁓—

People are people, and words are mixed with goodness and evilness. We don't know what was said, but we know what they did. Peoples' actions show what they believe. We know no one welcomed Ruth. As the Bible records, "She went to glean alone." She apparently had no direction. No one spoke to her, welcomed her, or helped her. She started gleaning by herself and ended in Boaz's field.

We know it was dangerous for a single woman to glean by herself because of Boaz's remarks to Ruth.

Boaz hears the stories, and he has compassion for Ruth. He knows how his mother, Rahab, is treated. He knows that without protection, Ruth could be beaten, robbed, or raped. He warns his servants both male and female not to hurt or rebuke Ruth. He invites her to sit and eat with him and his servants. He tells Ruth not to go into another's field. Boaz is a wealthy and prominent man, and his servants obey him.

The Bible does not speak of it, but Boaz has a wife. The buzz about town would reach that household also. She wouldn't have to gather water, but her servant girls do. And she would have other sources; she would know what was happening in Bethlehem.

—ᴍ—

So, when Boaz returns home:

"Boaz, dear, I hear the Moabitess that Naomi dragged back was gleaning in our fields. And furthermore, she ate with you and our servants. Is that so?"

"Yes, she ate with us. And I told her not to go into another's field. Her father-in-law, Elimelech, was a close relative. Shouldn't I protect his wife and daughter-in-law?" Boaz replies.

"Yes, if that is all you are doing," she says as she rolls her eyes.

"What do you mean?" he replies, quite puzzled.

"I mean, I heard she was a pretty young thing. You had better not have other interests. That was not our agreement. You got a large dowry for me—for me alone," she snaps, wrinkles her nose, and points her polished finger at him.

He throws his head back, and rolls his eyes, "That, I know; you remind me often."

"I am protecting our children—dear," she says as she turns her head away from him.

Boaz reaches out to touch and reassure her, but she turns on her heel and walks away from him.

He is left with his arm outstretched in the air, and that feeling again—that feeling of loneliness.

—ᵐ—

Boaz always watches the workers in his fields. He sees Ruth daily, gleaning in his fields. She is a good worker. He notices that Ruth does not crowd or try to get the most grain. He instructs his workers to leave extra sheaves of grain for her if she is gleaning behind them.

But what Ruth does amazes him. Ruth shares the bounty he orders for her with other gleaners. They did not welcome her, but she blesses them anyway. She is so unlike his wife and other greedy people.

At the end of the day, Boaz watches as Naomi comes to see Ruth. Ruth greets her with a tender hug and a soft kiss on the cheek.

He thinks it would be nice to be greeted with affection. He recalls his feelings of rejection, the feeling he had when his wife turned from him and walked away. She always leaves his arms empty.

As Ruth hugs Naomi, Naomi can see Boaz watching. She recognizes his look—the look of desire for compassion. He wants the kind of compassion that Ruth freely gives.

Naomi sees it with her eyes, but it is her heart that tells her Boaz has feelings for Ruth. Naomi begins to make plans.

Boaz does have feelings for Ruth; the feelings start out with protection, then admiration.

He notices during lunch how she smiles at a wildflower and laughs at a bird's antics. She appreciates even a sparse tree near them and gives thanks to it for offering its shade. The small tree offers only the scantest shade. This makes him laugh. His wife would have cursed it for how little it offered. He looks forward to seeing Ruth daily and enjoys her gratitude and cheerfulness.

When the harvesting is done, there will be the celebration. Naomi puts her plan into action.

"Ruth, you do like Boaz, don't you?" Naomi asks.

Some of the kinder women talk to Ruth now, and she is aware of some information. "Yes, Naomi, but he has a wife—one very possessive of him—and some kind of legal matter holding him."

Naomi knew more, though. "Let me tell you about the kinsman redeemer. By tradition, when a married man dies, leaving no son, his closest relative takes her to be his wife. If I had another son, Ruth, I would have given him to you. Then when a son is conceived, he is considered the first born of the one who died. The closest relative is the kinsman redeemer. If other children are born, they belong to the kinsman's line. If Boaz becomes your redeemer, the first son would be our family line. Elimelech's line would continue through him. Boaz is not the closest, though. It is Elimelech's brother; he knows it is beyond him, as he is in his last years. I have sought a counselor who will play his part when the time comes. I think Boaz just needs a little push to get him to admit to himself that this is what he wants. Now, this is what you are to do first."

"You have been gleaning in his fields, and you are invited to the harvest celebration. You will go, remain quiet, and watch only in the background. The men all drink, sing, celebrate until they are exhausted and fall asleep in a corner of the barn. Drinking with him would be flirting, cheapening yourself. You will show him respect and kindness. When he falls to sleep, you won't lie beside him as a prostitute or easy lady. You will lie at his feet. You will uncover his feet from the blanket and cover them with your skirt. This will show your willingness to care for his needs, even without being asked. He is not accustomed to kindness. You do desire to love and care for him, don't you, Ruth?" Naomi inquires.

"Yes, Naomi, I do; he is both kind and honorable. I do want him to be my kinsman redeemer. I will do as you say, and we will let God guide our future," Ruth says in agreement.

All during the celebration, Boaz sees Ruth in the background, sitting quietly. Although there is a crowd, she always catches his eye.

He wishes he could sing with her or talk to her. He wishes she were happy and dancing; he wishes he were dancing with her. He does not want to go home to his bitter wife. He continues to drink away his sorrows. His plan is to drink and drink some more and do no more thinking. He continues this until, as Naomi foretold, he lies down and passes out, dreaming of better times.

During the still hours of the night, Ruth approaches him. She stands at his feet and observes him—drunk, smelly, snoring loudly, with drool coming from the side of his mouth. She smiles and chuckles.

She speaks to God, "Yes, Lord, I love him even like that. Even in his most inglorious repose. I know this is not his true self. I do respect him. I wish to comfort and protect him. If it be your will, let this show him as Naomi has said."

She uncovers his feet, lies down by them, and covers his bare feet with her skirt.

When Boaz awakes, his throat is dry, and his breath is so bad he can taste the stench of it. In addition, his head really hurts. He braces himself up on one elbow and sees her. He is cut to the quick. His heart nearly stops. She is more beautiful than he ever imagined.

Ruth, with her quiet beauty and caring ways, hits his heart in a place it has never been.

Whether it is God who speaks to him or whether it is his own heart, it makes no difference. He knows. He knows what he must do, and he knows what he will do. He will marry this woman—this beautiful lady, this charming girl. He will redeem her.

Boaz meets publicly with the closest kinsman and offers him the first chance to redeem Ruth. Boaz is pleased because the man declines. Boaz then declares he will redeem Ruth.

Boaz marries Ruth, becoming her kinsman redeemer. They have one son, Obed. Obed is the father to Jesse, David's father.

—⟨⟩—

Many would consider Obed a half-breed because his mother is a Moabitess, not a Hebrew. And on his father's side, Boaz's mother, Rahab, his grandmother was a prostitute from Jericho. Rahab was not a Hebrew, either.

Jesse, David's father, is Obed's son. Jesse loves and respects his grandma, Ruth. He would be buried beside her. But that doesn't mean he isn't teased about her being a Moabitess.

If Ruth had been ridiculed, wouldn't Jesse have been aware of that? Not all people are kind. Wouldn't some people have ridiculed Jesse? If he had been ridiculed about Ruth being a Moabitess, could he have seen a son with reddish complexion as someone who would start that talk all over again? Would David's red complexion make people think of the red Esau, Edomites, and Moabites who were not born of Jacob—not Israelites?

Moab and Edom are not part of the twelve tribes of Israel.

Will people say David is part Moabite or part Edomite? Will they remember Jesse's family history and say, "Well, obviously this red stuff is coming from his side of the family?"

It's possible that David is purposely sent out-of-sight, out-of-mind, to tend the sheep. The dirt may have covered some of his ruddish complexion. And besides, maybe this redhead is from his wife's side. No one knows what is on Jesse's mind. We don't know why Jesse deliberately leaves David behind when Samuel instructs him to bring all his sons to the sacrifice.

—〜—

Now, we all have been slighted, insulted, and called mean names. We cannot control what other people say. But we do not need to keep repeating mean names or calling ourselves by these names.

When I do that, it cripples me. I cannot do what God has called me to do.

David, a man after God's own heart, listened to what God called him, and he wrote:

13 For You formed my inward parts;
You wove me in my mother's womb.
14 I will give thanks to You,
for I am fearfully and wonderfully made;

Wonderful are Your works,
And my soul knows it well.
15 My frame was not hidden from You,
When I was made in secret,
And skillfully wrought in the depths of the earth;
16 Your eyes have seen my unformed substance;
And in Your book were written
The days that were ordained for me,
When as yet there was not one of them.
17 How precious are Your thoughts to me, O God!
How vast is the sum of them!
18 If I should count them, they would outnumber
the sand.
When I awake, I am still with You.
19 O that You would slay the wicked, O God;
Depart from me, therefore, men of bloodshed.
20 For they speak against You, wickedly,
And Your enemies take Your name in vain.
21 Do I not hate those who hate You, O Lord?
And do I not loathe those who rise up against You?
22 I hate them with the utmost hatred;
They have become my enemies.
23 Search me, O God, and know my heart;
Try me and know my anxious thoughts;
24 And see if there be any hurtful way in me,
And lead me in the everlasting way.

Psalm 139:13-24

David not only sees himself fearfully and wonderfully made, but he also thanks God for it.

He is not thinking of what his brothers or father or others think of him. David is thinking on what

God thinks of him. His identity is that he is one of God's people. God loves him, and he loves God. He asks God to lead him.

—m—

My lowest point was going through a second divorce. During this marriage, I started attending a Christian church in Oglesby, Illinois. And I readily accepted the salvation that Jesus offers. I had not understood it before. I had prayed the salvation prayer at age nine, but I guess I did not understand salvation because I continued to carry all the burdens and shame of my past sins. I believed Jesus died for everyone, and we didn't need to do anything. We all were saved, but I didn't believe I was forgiven. I felt I was a loser, and I was ashamed.

Then I heard the analogy that it was like someone buying me a ticket for an airplane. I had to take the ticket and get on the plane, or I wasn't going anywhere.

Jesus offered to take the punishment for our sins, but we must accept it.

I could accept that Jesus died a horrible death, and that his death would pay the penalty for any and all my sins. I could accept that Jesus was God, who came from heaven down to Earth. I could accept he ascended from the grave and sits with Father God in heaven.

It was hard, but I finally accepted the belief that his sacrifice had paid for my sins. I couldn't add anything to his forgiveness, and adding guilt was like denying my salvation.

At last, I understood!

I thanked Jesus then, and I felt better about myself. I really was saved and completely forgiven, and there was nothing I could or needed to do to add to it.

I punched my ticket and got on that plane to forgiveness. And I left behind the land of shame and guilt.

—m—

My favorite hymn was "The Wonderful Grace of Jesus," written by Haldor Lillenas in 1918. He sold the rights for $5.00 to Hope Publishing Co.

The Wonderful Grace of Jesus

Wonderful grace of Jesus
Greater than all my sin
How shall my tongue describe it?
Where shall its praise begin?
Taking away my burden,
Setting my spirit free
For the wonderful grace of Jesus reaches me.

(Chorus)

Wonderful the matchless grace of Jesus
Deeper than the mighty rolling sea
Higher than the mountain
Sparkling like a fountain
All sufficient grace for even me.
Broader than the scope of my transgression
Greater far than all my sin and shame
O magnify the precious name of Jesus
Praise His name!

—⁓—

I got rid of the burden of past sins, but it did not stop troubles at home.

The second divorce was another failure. Again, I felt like killing myself. The whole atmosphere was very oppressive and negative. We all were unhappy. Even my children were ready to leave.

I packed up, took my children, and left. I couldn't kill myself; I had to take care of them.

We went to a Christian campground, and we were received with mixed messages. Some gave us blessings; others tried to sweep us under the rug.

My ex-husband and I did try reconciliation, but it did not take. Over a year later, divorce number two caused me to feel like a double failure. And there were plenty of people, some disguised as family and friends, who were quick to point it out to me.

But whatever I did wrong, I now knew, God forgave me. People might not, but God did. I went to church and took my children. I knew it was the place to be.

Over a year later, I was feeling lonely. I asked for my pastor's counsel about dating. At that time, my ex-husband was in a new relationship, and I wanted to move ahead too.

Wisely, the pastor prayed about it. He told me that God had shown him a picture of me, and it was a broken picture with cracks all throughout it. Remember all the cracks from my first marriage? He felt that I had Biblical grounds to date or remarry, but I did not have a whole person to offer someone. He felt I needed to heal before getting into another relationship.

He was right. I did not have a whole person to offer, and another person could not put me back together. That would have been too much to expect of anyone. I needed to get healing from God.

I did not like that answer, but I was mature enough to accept it. I had faith enough to carry on, be a mom, work as a nurse, and work on me.

—m—

Jesus Talks to Me

I respect and love you, child,
So much that I died for you!
What more can I offer?
What more can I do?

You are not done in part or error,
You are fully made anew!
Without blemish, without blame,
There is an entirely new you!

A purpose for your life,
And the strength to carry it through,
Are two more of the gifts
I freely give to you.

Thank you, Jesus.
I love you, too!
I owe you more than
I can ever repay to you.

Help me, Dear Lord
To do this thing for You—
To do things for others,
As gifts I give back to You!

Study questions:

Do you see yourself as fearfully and wonderfully made?

Are you one of God's people?

Do you believe Jesus died for your sins and you are forgiven?

Do you need to forgive yourself?

What are you doing to carry on?

What really is a foreigner—if you are one of God's people?

Are we hanging with God's people or foreigners?

How can we listen more to God, instead of people?

PART II
RELATIONSHIPS WITH GOD

4
TWO BOOKENDS: SAUL AND SAMUEL

BEFORE SAUL, ISRAEL has no kings. They have leaders, judges, and God.

Although Saul's journey as king can be a whole story, I will shorten it to set the stage for how this affects David.

During this time, the people have many battles with the Philistines. The Philistines had long before arrived by boat to the land of Israel. They are a warring people. The Philistines settle along the coast, but they keep pushing east, setting up or conquering more cities. There is constant war between the Philistines and the tribes of Israel.

Before Saul is made the king, the tribes of Israel have Samuel, the judge, who leads them. Samuel asks God for direction. Then he informs the people what God had told him. With God's direction, Israeli battles are won. It does not matter if they are outnumbered or facing huge armies with superior weaponry. At times, God wipes the enemy out in front of them.

Despite the wonders God has worked for them, the Israeli people request a king like other places. Neither God nor Samuel approves. In fact, God says he is their king, and the people reject him.

God warns the people how a king would impose stiff laws and demands on them and that the new king would mandate acceptance of his new laws and rules.

Samuel speaks for God, telling the people that God is warning that a king would do these things which would be unpleasant for them:

- He would take their sons from them and place them in his service.

- He would appoint commanders to do his plowing and make weapons of war.

- He would take their daughters for perfumers, cooks, and bakers.

- He would take the best of their fields and give it to his servants.

- He would take a tenth of their produce.

- He would take their servants to become his servants.

- He would take a tenth of their flocks.

But the people clamor, "Give us a king like other nations!"

> 18 "Then you will cry out in that day, because of your king whom you have chosen for yourselves, but the Lord will not answer you in that day."
> 19 Nevertheless, the people refused to listen to the voice of Samuel, and they said, "No, but there shall be a king over us,
> 20 that we also may be like all the nations, that our king may judge us and go out before us and fight our battles."
>
> —1 Samuel 8:18-20

The people not only reject God as king but also reject Samuel as their judge.

Since the people insist upon having a king, God chooses the best available at that time—Saul. Saul is strong; he is head and shoulders taller than other men. He is approximately thirty years old.

Samuel tells Saul in private that he is God's choice and anoints him king. However, when it comes time to announce Saul as king publicly, he hides.

Israel's new king, an adult man, there with his family, standing head and shoulders above others, hides among the baggage.

However, Saul cannot hide from God. God tells Samuel where to find Saul. Samuel brings Saul in front of the Israelites and proclaims him as king.

So, Saul does not start out by putting himself forward. In fact, he is fearful.

Since at first Saul doesn't trust in himself, he listens and follows instructions from Samuel and God. And with Samuel's and God's guidance, Saul learns to become a warrior and a king. And the people's confidence in him grows.

Unfortunately, over the years, Saul begins to believe in himself too much.

Saul foresees his kingdom as everlasting. He plans on his oldest son, Jonathan, becoming the next king. He sees his kingdom as secure, passing through his family, generation after generation.

Instead of shy or backward, Saul has become very forward. He's become proud and self-sufficient. His actions show he thinks he has the right to perform both blessings and curses.

—⁂—

During one battle, Saul proclaims a curse on any man who eats before sundown. Saul's curse includes a death penalty to anyone who disavows his order.

However, at that time, Jonathan is busy fighting and does not hear the curse. After hours of fighting and near exhaustion, Jonathan finds a honeycomb.

He dips his staff in the honey and tastes it, and it refreshes him.

The battle is won, but later, Jonathan is found guilty. It does not matter that Jonathan was unaware of the curse. The people beg Saul not to kill Jonathan. Although Saul relents and lets Jonathan live, he still has cursed his own son.

Saul does not see that God should be the one in charge of both blessings and curses. Saul does not repent. Saul still sees himself as self-sufficient— next time as a priest.

—⁂—

Later, after winning a different battle, Saul grows tired of waiting for Samuel. After all victories, Samuel offers a sacrifice in thanksgiving to God. Saul has seen the sacrifice done many times. He becomes tired of waiting for Samuel and offers the sacrifice himself.

This is wrong because Saul is not a priest. Offering the sacrifice is a priestly duty.

Samuel arrives after Saul has offered the sacrifice. Samuel is angry, and he prophesies the demise of Saul's kingdom.

13 And Samuel said to Saul, "You have acted foolishly, you have not kept the commandment of the Lord your God, which He commanded you, for now the Lord would have established your kingdom over Israel forever.

14 But now your kingdom shall not endure. The
Lord has sought out for Himself a man after His
own heart, and the Lord has appointed him as
ruler over His people because you have not kept
what the Lord commanded you."
—1 Samuel 13:13,14

Saul apologizes and asks Samuel to pray for him.

Saul thinks saying he is sorry is enough to take
care of his faux pas.

However, Saul is unrepentant; later, he commits
the same transgression.

In a later battle, the Israelites are at war with
King Agag. God instructs them to keep no spoils
and kill everyone, including King Agag.

The Israelites are victorious. But a second time,
Saul grows tired of waiting for Samuel, to come
and offer the thanksgiving sacrifice. Saul again
offers the sacrifice.

Saul also ignores God's instructions.

Both he and the soldiers keep the spoils. They
have sheep, other animals, and trophies. In addition,
Saul spares King Agag.

When Samuel arrives, he sees the smoke from
the sacrifice. He hears the bleating of sheep and
sees King Agag.

This is the final straw. God rejects Saul.

22 Samuel said, "Has the Lord as much delight
in burnt offerings and as in obeying the voice of

the Lord? Behold, to obey is better than sacrifice,
and to heed than the fat of rams.
23 For rebellion is the sin of divination, and
insubordination is as iniquity and idolatry.
Because you have rejected the word of the Lord,
He has also rejected you from being king."

—1 Samuel 15:22, 23

Samuel demands Agag be brought to him.

But Samuel said, "As your sword has made
women childless, so shall your mother be childless among women." And Samuel hewed Agag
to pieces before the Lord at Gigal.

—1 Samuel 15: 33

Samuel turns to leave. Saul, trying to keep
Samuel from leaving, grabs Samuel's robe, and it
tears. Samuel turns to Saul and gives the prophecy
that Saul's kingdom is also torn from him and given
to his neighbor.

Saul has always had Samuel with him as his
counselor and advisor. But this time, Samuel does
not go with Saul to his fortress in Gibeah. Samuel
goes to his own home in Ramah. For the rest of
Samuel's life, he will not counsel Saul. However,
after Samuel's death, Saul will summon Samuel's
spirit. Saul knows this is also against God's law.

And for Samuel, although he leaves to his own
home, it is hard for him to see Saul fail. Samuel
leaves, but he grieves for Saul. Samuel's grief

continues until God speaks to him, commanding him to anoint a new king.

> 1 Now the Lord said to Samuel, "How long will you grieve over Saul, since I have rejected him from being king over Israel? Fill your horn with oil and go; I will send you to Jesse the Bethlehemite, for I have selected a king for Myself among his sons,"
> 2 But Samuel said, "How can I go? When Saul hears of it, he will kill me." And the Lord said, "Take a heifer with you and say, 'I have come to sacrifice to the Lord.'
> 3 "You shall invite Jesse to the sacrifice, and I will show you what you shall do; and you shall anoint for Me the one whom I designate to you."
> —1 Samuel 16: 1-3

Even before he is born, Samuel's mother dedicates him to God. Samuel grows up with the priests and becomes God's spokesperson at a very young age. He sees and prophesies about God's amazing miracles. He is a faithful judge over the people. Samuel can hear God's voice. He knows God is faithful and tells the truth, but Samuel is not a robot. He has human feelings.

The scripture tells us he grieves for Saul. He is afraid of Saul. Samuel says to God, "Saul will kill me."

He is angry Agag is still alive, and he hews him to pieces. He is a father, and when he hears his sons are not faithful, he is sad. Although he can hear God's voice, Samuel still has human feelings—feelings of doubt, sadness, and fear. But Samuel is faithful and overcomes his feelings.

Samuel follows God's instructions.

Saul, on the other hand, starts out fearful, afraid, and self-doubting, but somewhere along the line, he becomes self-sufficient, proud, and unfaithful. In the end, Saul does things his own way.

That's when God can no longer use Saul.

—⁓—

You have heard the saying, "Out of the frying pan into the fire." For me, it was out of the church (where I was somewhat accepted/somewhat rejected) into the prison. Not that I was arrested and convicted—I applied for work and won the job!

I had dropped out of high school during the last semester of my senior year, but I had also continued to fill in the blanks. I received my GED that same year and started night college classes. A year later, I started college full time.

After my second marriage and second child, I was a part-time college student again. A mere nine years later, I graduated with my Associate Degree in Nursing, which entitled me to become a registered nurse (RN) after passing my state board exams.

Now in my thirties, I was an RN with a new job at a state prison, and since my second divorce, I had not been dating. I had been trying to 'be a mom' and 'put myself back together.' I had been a third wheel with my best friend Tammy and her husband, Alan. My children were welcomed at their home. We did many fun things together. Her husband, Alan, worked in the prison and had told me about this nurse's job there. It was a full-time job with good benefits.

When I started working there, I found out that not everyone in prison is terrible, and not everyone on the outside is good. In fact, I should have been looking at people as either believers in God or non-believers.

I started dating, and it was full of its own diffi-culties. The first date was with someone I thought was a Christian. He said he was in a bad relation-ship and was going to break up with his girlfriend.

As it turned out, he never broke up with her. Instead, he bought her a diamond. Obviously, that was the end of dating him.

Next, I dated someone too young, too wild. He was known for drinking alcohol heavily. I thought we were so opposite; I laughed when he asked me out.

Later, I felt I had definitely managed that badly. So, I asked him if he was serious. He said he was serious—until I laughed. I apologized and accepted the date. It turned out, to my surprise, I liked him—a lot. It really did not work out, though. After a few months of dating, he gave up on the relationship. The ending of that relationship was another low point in my life.

I was very angry with God. I asked, "If God is love, what is this all about?" I felt very unloved. My ex-husband had remarried, which added to my frustration.

At the holiday function, my ex-boyfriend showed up with a date—another low blow. He definitely was moving on.

That night, I felt most rejected. I got in my car to go home, and I drove too fast and recklessly. I was trying to see if the new car would go 120 mph, even though the roads were covered with snow and ice. I got it over 90 and lost control. The right front tire veered off the road and hit something hard. It knocked the steering wheel from my hands. That should have sent me farther off or sent the car rolling. But it set me back on the road—no damage to my car.

I had a second chance to consider my decisions! After reflection, I knew dying wasn't going to change that relationship; it would only leave my children without a mother. I thanked God the car was righted and drove safely home.

I also thanked God that I had not hurt anyone else. I felt that an angel had thrown my car back on the road.

Every now and then, when I pass that part of the road, I look. And I still don't find anything I could have hit. I felt saved by God's grace.

After that night, I thought hard about that relationship. I tried to paint a picture in my mind, of the two of us living happily ever after—some way I could safely raise my two children. I could not even imagine a life together for us. It really was not going to work out.

I needed someone who wanted a family, someone who also was a Christian.

A young friend once told me that in her life, the devil first sent her the wrong guy. And the wrong guy, in many respects, was a lot like the right guy. She had to let go of the wrong guy, though, before she could meet the right one.

Many times, I have been stuck in my life because I did not want to let go of something that was wrong for me.

I decided this time that I had to carry on. He knew we were not a match. It was time; I accepted it.

I met my husband, Kenny, in prison. He also worked there. He also was younger, a big man, and a drinker.

We worked the same shift but not usually in the same department. One night after my break-up, he was assigned to the health department. That night, I was working alone.

In my boredom, I had been shooting rubber bands at a target. (I had finished my work, and it was the night shift. I was keeping busy to stay awake—that's my excuse). Kenny came from his end of the department to check out the noise, then casually asked about my boyfriend. I said we were no longer dating. He turned to leave and said, "God works in mysterious ways."

I watched him walk away, and the question to myself was, "Hmm, he's a Christian?" I never would have guessed it.

He also made the cut later when I decided I should try dating again. I ran the prospects' names past Alan, my best friend's husband. We were working at the same prison, and the men on the list were co-workers. I figured he knew the guys better than I did.

Alan looked at my list and laughed. Then he started telling me, "Not that one," (and why). Soon all the names were scratched off except one. Kenny was the only one who made the cut.

It turns out that Kenny was (and is) a Christian. And he was ready to put away his wild lifestyle and have a family. We dated for eighteen months before we got engaged. Later that year, we tied the knot and have been married thirty-two years. We have two daughters.

When the first dating relationships were a bust, I felt like giving up. I cared for someone who wanted to break it off, and I felt like committing suicide. I realized suicide was not the answer. If I hated my life, I needed to change it. If I wanted God's blessings, I had to lean on God for direction. I had to give up trying to do it my way.

But when I learned to carry on, things did get better.

When I let go of the wrong one, I found someone who also cared for me. Kenny and I are still married after all these years.

Grace Is

Grace is
>God providing forgiveness for me
>Before I committed, confessed
>Or turned away from my sins.

Grace is
>God loving me
>Even though I couldn't
>Love myself.

Grace is
>God calling me
>Even though
>I was not listening.

Grace is
>God's plan for me,
>When I am ready
>To receive it.

Grace is
>God's free gift
>His gift
>That I never deserved.

Study questions:

God can use us afraid or with doubt.

God continued to use Samuel for the rest of his life.

God protected Samuel from Saul.

God also protected the man he picked, David, a man after His own heart, from Saul.

How do you think God is using you?

Have you ever felt God is not there for you?

Is there something you feel God wants you to do, but you are afraid?

5
WHAT IS A MAN AFTER GOD'S OWN HEART?

DAVID IS PROBABLY thirteen to fifteen years old when God sends Samuel to anoint him. That's not what we usually consider a man. In the Jewish tradition, boys at age thirteen celebrate their Bar Mitzvahs. It is considered the age of accountability.

We can see into David's heart by reading his Psalms. The Psalms are not necessarily written before he is anointed, but the thoughts and feelings toward God are already there in his heart.

He expresses thankfulness to God.

> 1 I will give thanks to the Lord with all my heart; I will tell of all Your wonders.
> 2 I will be glad and exult in You; I will sing praise to Your name, O Most High.
> —Psalm 9: 1, 2

He acknowledges that God is the highest and even names God *Most High*. In other words, David sees no one above God.

David expresses his love to God and recognizes that God is the source of his strength.

I love You, O Lord, my strength.

—Psalm 18: 1

David acknowledges God as the Creator of Heaven and Earth. He extols the glory of God and of creation and defines man's position in the creation.

1 O Lord, our Lord, how majestic is Your name in all the earth, who have displayed Your splendor above the heavens!
2 From the mouth of infants and nursing babes You have established strength because of Your adversaries, to make the enemy and the revengeful cease.
3 When I consider Your heavens, the work of Your fingers, the moon and the stars, which You have ordained;
4 What is man that You take thought of him, and the son of man that You care for him?
Yet you have made him a little lower than God, and You crown him with glory and majesty!
6 You make him to rule over the works of Your hands; You have put all things under his feet,
7 all sheep and oxen, and also the beasts of the field,

8 the birds of the heavens and the fish of the sea,
whatever passes through the paths of the seas.
9 O Lord, our Lord, how majestic is Your name
in all the earth!

—Psalm 8:1-9

God is David's refuge and the one in whom he
trusts.

David praises God with his family and in public.

I will tell of Your name to my brethren; In the
midst of the assembly I will praise You.

—Psalm 22: 22

—〰—

I have not always given credit to God or loved him as I should. Sometimes I am sure people did not know that I was a believer. There may be people reading this today who have known me and are totally surprised at my thoughts and beliefs.

In writing poetry, I would write down the thoughts as they ran through my mind. However, I would not share it with anyone because I was sure my thoughts and poems were not good.

In the Bible story of the talents, we learn that God gives a different portion to different people. Whether we have one talent or ten, we are supposed to use what we are given.

So now I am sharing my poems. Maybe it is only a tenth of one talent, maybe more, but I will share them. I hope it will encourage you to share something you felt was not good enough.

Writing my feelings out is one way I carry on.

Portions of Love

Lord, without you,
  I am nothing.
Without your Grace,
  I am lost.
Without your touch,
  I am empty.
Without your spirit,
  I am lifeless.
Without your blood,
  I am filthy.

Lord
  Cleanse me,
  Fill me,
  Renew my spirit,
  Make me, mold me,
  Into your plan.

I give you
  My dreams,
  My hopes
  My plans.

Shatter them, scatter them,
  Destroy them, if You wish.
  Give to me the portion
  That You set aside for me.

In that portion,
  I will rejoice with You.
  I am Your servant.
  Portion to me as You choose.

Study questions:

What is a man or woman after God's own heart?

In what ways did David honor God?

Samuel wasn't perfect. David wasn't perfect. Do we need to be perfect to honor God?

Was Rahab and Ruth's purpose in life to demonstrate faith and loyalty to their family?

Do you believe God loves you?

Are you trying to be a person after God's own heart?

6
THE ANOINTING OF DAVID

SAMUEL WILL ANOINT David as God's choice for the next king. Anointing is common practice; even animals were anointed. It is used for cleansing and healing. Even the anointing of a person is not necessary to make him a king. In the book of Kings, one anointing is for the next king, and a second and different anointing is for a priest.

Because Samuel is anointing someone does not necessarily mean they are God's choice to be the next king. Did David or his family understand what Samuel's anointing of David meant?

—⁊⁊—

Samuel is recognized as he enters Bethlehem. The word spreads quickly—*the judge Samuel has come to Bethlehem.*

The people are terrorized. They wonder, *what could they have done?* They scurry from the water hole, and people hide in their homes.

The elders are afraid and attentively approach Samuel.

A leader speaks up, "Is there something we have done wrong that brings you to our village, Samuel?"

Samuel repeats the plan God gave him. "No, I have come to make a sacrifice. I am consecrating you elders and Jesse and all of his sons to attend the sacrifice."

There is a buzz and excitement in all of Bethlehem.

Jesse cannot wait to tell his wife and daughters. "Samuel is here."

His wife, like others, is afraid. "What have we done?"

Jesse laughs. "Nothing bad. He is here to offer a sacrifice. And he has asked me and all our sons to attend!"

"Oh my, Samuel has set aside our family to attend. When is this to be? We will have to mend and wash the clothing and get them all presentable for Samuel," she says.

She is already looking for needle and thread in case someone's clothing has torn.

He also has four grandsons, Abishai, Joab, Asahel—from his eldest daughter, Zeruiah; his fourth grandson is Amasa, from his younger daughter, Abigail. Amasa's father is Jether, the Ishmaelite.

Zeruiah, his oldest daughter, adds, "Well, my sons are sons of yours also. I will make them presentable too. I would not want them to miss out on this. Has Samuel ever sacrificed in Bethlehem before?"

Jesse replies, "He has never been here in my life or any time I remember. Something big must be about to happen here." The boys are all gathered shortly, and the process begins:

- checking clothing and sandals and repairing as needed

- cleaning dirt from behind the ears, under fingernails, and under chins

- brushing hair and tying it in place

As his wife hurries, cleaning up the boys, she notices there is no David. She asks, "Has someone sent for David? I know he is not far away."

Jesse answers, "I didn't send for him; he's with the sheep."

"He is also your son, and a servant could be sent to watch the sheep!" she snaps.

Jesse shrugs. "I don't think all the scrubbing in the world would make him presentable to one such as Samuel. Seriously, dear, he would be an embarrassment."

She does not agree, but she can see his mind is set, and David will be left out. The only thing she can say is a warning, "It is never a good thing to try to fool a prophet."

"What do you mean?" he asks in astonishment.

"You told me Samuel consecrated you and all of your sons to attend the sacrifice. David is one of your sons!" she replies curtly as she continues preparing the boys.

The boys know better than to add their thoughts to this discussion. But some of them agree with their father; David would be an embarrassment. He would be dirty and noisome from attending the sheep.

David is out with his sheep, and probably is totally unaware of the discussion at home concerning him.

However, his nephew Asahel is fast and loves to run. Earlier in the day, he ran to tell David that Samuel is here to offer a sacrifice. Now David has moved his flock close enough to see.

The family is brought before Samuel.

6 When they entered, he looked at Eliab and thought, "Surely the Lord's anointed is before Him."

7 But the Lord said to Samuel, "Do not look at his appearance or at the height of his stature, because I have rejected him; for God sees not as man sees, for man looks at the outward appearance, but the Lord looks at the heart."

8 Then Jesse called Abinadab and made him pass before Samuel. And he said, "The Lord has not chosen this one either."

9 Next Jesse made Shammah pass by. And he said, "The Lord has not chosen this one either."

10 Thus Jesse made seven of his sons pass before Samuel. But Samuel said to Jesse, "The Lord has not chosen these."

11 And Samuel said to Jesse, "Are these all the children?" And he said, "There remains yet the youngest, and behold, he is tending the sheep." Then Samuel said to Jesse, "Send and bring him; for we will not sit down until he comes here."

12 So he sent and brought him in. Now, he was ruddy, with beautiful eyes and a handsome appearance. And the Lord said, "Arise, anoint him; for this is he."

13 Then Samuel took the horn of oil and anointed him in the midst of his brothers; and the Spirit of the Lord came mightily upon David from that day forward. And Samuel arose and went to Ramah.

—1 Samuel 16:6-13

The scripture does not say whether Samuel announced that he was anointing David the next king. The scripture does say Samuel felt that Saul would kill him to stop him from anointing another king. Apparently, neither David nor his family knew what the anointing meant.

If Samuel had announced he was anointing David the new king, Saul would have tried to kill David then.

Samuel left the announcement to God to deliver it in His time.

David's brothers and parents are there at the anointing, and they aren't saluting David. They are treating him the same as they did before the anointing. After this anointing, David is still the family shepherd.

But David is not the same.

The spirit of the Lord immediately rests upon David, and the things David excels in are magnified. David loves music, and his singing is now better than ever. Some of the Psalms he wrote are for flute, which would be a shepherd's musical tool. Were these his earlier Psalms?

David is also known for playing the harp. Does he excel musically, so that he needs a harp? Does he invest in one for himself, or does his family invest in a harp for him?

Someone does; he has a harp.

And he is known for his singing. Later, he will be asked to play his harp and sing for King Saul. The spirit of God that helps David excel is the same spirit that rested upon Saul. It was God's spirit that helped Saul excel as a warrior and Israel's king.

However, when God sends his Holy Spirit to David, he removes the Holy Spirit from Saul.

Now Saul is grieving over the absence of the spirit of God. He misses the power. He wants the power back, and he is angry and depressed.

—ɱ—

I know at times I have been like Saul. I chose to do it my own way.

At other times, I ask God for guidance, but that does not mean I follow his advice.

Sometimes I cannot understand his answer or do not hear an answer.

Sometimes I choose to do what is wrong. I am a sinner; we all are.

I know I do not fully understand the Holy Spirit and how or when it descends on someone. Nor do I understand how it affects them. I know the Holy Spirit exists; when It comes into one's life, we are surely changed. Since the changes are from God, the changes are good.

I know there are evil spirits too. We need to be careful about what we ask into our lives. Ouija boards, seances, and fortune telling with cards are only a few of the things I thought were for amusement. Being tormented by evil spirits is not amusing. They do exist. If you have or are involved with any of these or other occult things, repent and ask for God's protection and forgiveness.

Make sure your prayers are to God and wait for his answers. If you feel you do not know God's answer, start with action and let him steer you.

That is what I do when I carry on.

Empty Hands

My God and Father,
How I love You so,
I long to be there with You,
And roam the earth no more.

I fear I have done so poorly,
When in Your presence I stand,
I'll have no gift to offer You;
I'll be there with empty hands.

Please give me the courage
To use the gifts You gave.
So, when in Your presence I stand
I'll hold a gift—
And not have empty hands.

Study questions:

Have you ever been angry or jealous of somebody else's talent or gifts?

Do you thank God for what you have? Your abilities? Your talents? Your knowledge? Your home? Your family?

Or do you look at what you do not have?

Are you a good example for your family? Your neighbors? Your friends?

When things go well, do you give yourself or God the credit?

When you make errors, do you make excuses, or do you apologize?

Are you more like Saul or David?

7
SAUL, THE UNREPENTANT HEART

DURING THE YEARS when God's spirit is resting on him, Saul did many good and powerful and masterful things. However, after years of success, he apparently begins to think he is powerful and in charge. In his later years, he does not always obey God's commands.

When Saul goes to fight King Agag, it is God's command to destroy all the people and keep no spoils. Saul must rationalize that some things, animals, or people are too good to destroy, and he ignores God's orders. We know he and the soldiers keep a lot of the plunder, and he lets King Agag live.

Why does he save Agag? Does Saul want to bring Agag before the people, so they will praise Saul for capturing him? Or does he believe that Agag could be an ally? We don't really know what Saul is thinking, but his actions are contrary to God's instructions.

Many years ago, when Saul was announced the first king, not all the people were for him. However, he was God's choice.

God sends his own Spirit to rest on Saul, and Samuel stays to guide him. With God's and Samuel's guidance, Saul has many victories. And the people's loyalty to him grows.

Now Samuel has left him; and God has taken away his Holy Spirit.

Saul has instead an evil spirit troubling him.

14 Now the Spirit of the Lord departed from Saul, and an evil spirit from the Lord terrorized him.
15 Saul's servants then said to him, "Behold now, an evil spirit from God is terrorizing you.
16 Let our Lord now command your servants who are before you. Let them seek a man who is a skillful player on the harp; and it shall come about when the evil spirit from God is on you, that he shall play the harp with his hand, and you will be well."
17 So Saul said to his servants, "Provide for me now a man who can play well and bring him to me."
18 Then one of the young men said, "Behold, I have seen a son of Jesse the Bethlehemite who is a skillful musician, a mighty man of valor, a warrior, one prudent in speech, and a handsome man; and the Lord is with him.

19 So Saul sent messengers to Jesse and said, "Send me your son David who is with the flock." 20 Jesse took a donkey loaded with bread and a jug of wine and a young goat, and sent them to Saul by David his son. 21 Then David came to Saul and attended him; and Saul loved him greatly, and he became his armor bearer. 22 Saul sent to Jesse, saying, "Let David now stand before me, for he has found favor in my sight." 23 So it came about whenever the evil spirit from God came to Saul, David would take the harp and play it with his hand; and Saul would be refreshed and be well, and the evil spirit would depart from him.

—1 Samuel 16:14-23

—ᴧᴧᴧ—

My goal is to give clarity to the Bible, so that the reader will sense the truth of its stories. And I would like to ignore the last Bible verse. I am sure theologians have discussed it and come up with many long and intricate answers on how God sent an evil spirit. I keep in mind three things. God does not lie. God does not sin. The Bible is the true word of God.

Sending the evil spirit is not a sin since God does not sin. It does cause suffering and torment for Saul. Is there any good that could come from it?

If Saul is uncomfortable, maybe he will repent and ask for forgiveness. Isn't repentance and forgiveness more important to God than Saul's comfort? Is God only trying to correct Saul?

Attitudes and actions God might want to reprove:

- Pride—Twice Saul takes charge of the sacrifice.

- Glory-seeking—the glory for the victory should have been God's, not Saul's. Is Saul allowing the spoils of war kept, so the people with thank and praise him?

- Disobedience—Saul ignores God's directions.

There are some things Saul needs to learn about God. God is all-powerful and all-knowing, and redemption comes only from God.

It seems the evil spirit does not cause any life-threatening illnesses or injury. The evil spirit troubles Saul. But instead of humbling him to repent and ask for forgiveness, it makes him angry and drives him into a state of madness.

Saul chooses not to humble himself before God and repent. He chooses instead to disavow any wrong and continues with his self-promotion plans.

Saul's actions seem to be saying, "You can be my God only if your plans are my plans. I plan to remain king. I reject any plans from you, God, to replace me as king. I will do it my way."

Is the evil spirit replaying Samuel's words in Saul's ears?

The evil spirit could be saying, "Your kingdom is torn from you. God has chosen a new king, a man after God's own heart. Your kingdom is given to your neighbor!"

Is this the madness Saul is having? His mind cannot solve this riddle. *Who has God chosen to be the next king?*

Saul doesn't see that the problem is his actions and attitudes. He feels the other man who God has chosen is the problem.

Saul must think, *If I find that man and kill him, then my kingdom will be secure again. God can't replace me with a dead man.*

The Bible is described as a double-edged sword, and so is the evil spirit God has sent to Saul. The spirit could have been sent to encourage repentance and redemption. However, Saul rejects that. And God knew he would. So, instead, the evil spirit is used to bring the next king to Saul.

While Saul in his madness seeks comfort, he sends for a musician. David, the one who will be the next king, is there at Saul's request. The man Saul seeks to kill is the one he invites into his court.

Thus, David gets the king training firsthand. He has a chance to see what Saul does right and what he does wrong. He sees how Saul runs his government, commands an army, gathers good counselors, and provides justice and protection for the people.

David learns new skills and makes important alliances. These are things he could not do while shepherding.

Does David know at this time that he is to be the next king?

I don't think so; I don't think he knows yet.

—⚏—

My father was a painter, not an artist; he also did wallpapering. He had many ladders, and one day while working on our home, he decided to teach my older brother, Mike, how to climb up an extension ladder properly. Two ladders were held together with channels and locks so that they could be made longer together than either was originally. He had the extension ladder on the highest side of our house, and Mike got to climb up, get on the roof, and then climb back down. He did great; he had no fear. I said got to because that was how I felt. I wanted to do that.

I loved to climb. My grandmother told me that when I was only four or five, my mom would say, "Why don't you go outside and climb a tree?"

Apparently, sometimes I was underfoot and asking too many questions. Anyway, I remember being excited about climbing. Climbing trees was my favorite thing to do. My favorite tree was a mulberry tree that was only about twelve feet high. I could climb up and sit on the very top fork of the tree. This roost was probably eight or nine feet high, as a few skinny branches waved above my head. I would sit there for long periods, looking all around. I would imagine all kinds of stories. I'd talk to the birds, squirrels, trees, or my teddy bear. Whoever couldn't talk back would be a good choice.

As young as I remember, I believed in God. I don't remember ever not believing.

Also, I don't remember believing in Santa Claus. It made no sense to me.

My mother told a story about my brother and me. She said she always felt whenever we were old enough to ask if Santa was real, then we were old enough to know the truth. For my brother, it came when he went to first grade—age six. He came home one day upset and asked if Santa was real.

Mom replied, "No, he's not. Your dad and I give you presents. But don't spoil it for your sister."

She said it was like a light bulb going off; he brightened up and ran from the room. She knew he was running to ruin my day, so she was right behind him. I had turned three years old in the summer, and she wanted to save my belief.

Mike ran into the room, and announced from the doorway, "Mary, there's no Santa Claus!"

Mom said I looked up from playing and said, "There's no Easter Bunny, either."

She said he was all upset again, and I continued to sit and play quietly.

There was a lot of sibling rivalry in our family, even though it was only the two of us. He was always trying to ruin my day somehow. I guess he thought it was his job.

Now three years later, my brother got to climb way up and get on the roof. I was soon saying, "I want to climb up too."

It didn't take long for my dad to relent. He repeated all his instructions and told me, "You can climb up, but you can't get on the roof. You can just touch it."

I was excited but a little disappointed and jealous; I didn't get to match my brother's experience. But soon, I was up and down on that ladder, like a billy goat on a hill. I was not afraid but excited. Those were all good feelings: my sense of accomplishment, my dad's approval, and his pride in how well we climbed.

Evidently, my brother was also excited and looked forward to getting on that roof again too.

It was a while in coming. It was winter, and there was snow on the ground. My dad was at work, and my mom was going to get groceries. She felt it was okay to leave us playing in the yard. We lived in a small town, and the grocery store was only a few blocks away.

Mike, age nine, was three years older than I. Doug, Mike's friend, was also there. We were in coats and snow boots and playing outside in the yard. I was playing with my dog.

As soon as Mom left, Mike went into action. He got the small step ladder, brought it to the deck outside the kitchen, and he and Doug started climbing up on the roof.

The dog kept barking. I had to put her in the house. She was warning us that this was not a good idea.

My brother rarely included me, but this time he did. I suppose he didn't want me telling on him. I was excited he was including me. I was right behind them. Wow, on the roof!

This house had many roof levels; it was easy to get to the highest level. Double wow! I had a much bigger view than from my little tree.

The boys decided to jump down from that roof to the front porch roof, which was much larger. I followed, and we ran back and forth on that roof. When we decided to leave, we found out that none of us was tall enough to climb back up onto the big roof. Two of us with pushing and pulling could get there, but no two could pull up the third person. One person was always stuck.

The boys shoved me up with orders to go and find a rope. It was winter, and I was only six. I came back with a hose. I tried to push it up to them from the ground; it was stiff. I got the small stepladder; it was too short. I was really no help.

The snow was piled up on one side of the porch. I don't remember which boy, but one of the boys thought he could jump into it. He did, and that solved the problem of how to get the third person off the porch roof. Soon, the second boy jumped off.

They thought that was fun. They moved the step ladder back and climbed up to jump off the front porch roof again.

Well, it was too far for me to jump. I liked climbing, not jumping. So, I felt left out and came up with my own plan. "Hey, let's jump down on the little roof on the other side of the house. We can hang on the edge and shimmy down the post."

Mike told me that would not work and went to jump off the front porch again. I wasn't jumping, but I was sure I could climb down. I went and slid down onto the small porch roof on the west side of the house.

This roof was even farther from the roof above, and it was also father down to the ground. The little porch roof and the ground around it were covered with ice. There was no snow or snow drift to cushion a jump. And there was no way to hang on the edge and wrap my feet around the post as Mike had told me.

I couldn't get up or down. I yelled for the boys, and they did try to pull me up, but right then, Mom drove up. They took off before she could see them, and she had not seen me.

We had been hiding from Mom to have our great fun, which we knew was wrong. Now alone and helpless, I needed her. She often did not wait for Dad to get home; if we needed a swat, we got it.

There was a child's game with a paddle, a rubber band, and rubber ball. Eventually, the rubber band broke, and the game was over. She kept the paddle and could draw it out in a second and apply it to our learning curves.

It did not matter; I needed her. So, I hollered and yelled. I hollered for her. I hollered for my dog. I begged my dog to go and get her. I saw that on TV.

Dogs are good at getting help for kids who have gotten themselves into trouble.

It took some time. She was in the kitchen putting away groceries. She was too far away to hear me. The dog did hear me, came to a nearby window, and wagged her tail. I wanted barking, but she was content she found me. I sat on the roof, afraid to stand on the ice. I continued shouting, trying to make enough noise for Mom to hear.

When Mom did find me, there was a lot of yelling and scolding from her. But my mom was not a climber, and she didn't know how to get me down. She brought a ladder—too short. I know how she felt.

She decided the closest she could get to me was to open a very small window. She cut the screen and reached out to me. That meant I had to step on the icy roof, walk to the edge, and trust her to grab me. I did, and she did.

By then, I was so cold I was shaking. I don't think I could have felt the paddle. But this time, no paddle. She said those dreaded words, "Wait until your father gets home."

She put me in a warm bath first, and afterwards pajamas, and directed me to bed. She found my brother and scolded him, and he was to wait until Dad got home too.

It was scary facing my dad. I don't remember any other time that my mom thought the punishment due us was severe enough that my dad needed to administer it.

Now as an adult and wife, I wonder ... did she blame him for showing us how to climb ladders and get on the roof? And was this part of his punishment too?

However, as a child, I thought it was the former, and I was afraid.

That night it was like court; we were all to sit. Dad stood in front of us and talked. All our transgressions were laid out. Dad was speaking clearly and loudly, and for emphasis, he pointed his finger at us. All the terrible things that could have happened were listed, and my mom nodded in approval.

I don't know if we weren't allowed to talk or if we were too afraid. There was no excuse; we were guilty of all of it.

Then Dad said, "Mike, stand up, come here."

He made Mike stand in front of him and swung at him like he was going to slap Mike in the face. No one ever slapped us in the face. Not Dad, not Mom, no one. Mike ducked. Dad straightened Mike upright, and said, "You deserve this." Dad swung again, and again; Mike ducked. My eyes almost popped out of my head. He told Mike to sit down. "For now."

"Mary, you're next. Stand up here!"

I was so afraid, but I couldn't handle all the ducking, swinging, and repeating. I decided to just get it over. I stood still, waiting to be knocked across the room; I shut my eyes. My dad swung at me, and I did not move. He simply softly ticked my cheek. I opened my eyes. My dad took my head in his two hands, bent down, and kissed me on the forehead.

He said, "Don't ever do that again."

I got mercy—not the punishment I deserved. I had knowingly disobeyed. I was sorry, and my parents forgave me. Mike, after seeing I was not murdered, stood to receive the same mercy and forgiveness.

Isn't our great God like that? He sometimes gives us mercy and forgiveness instead of the punishment we deserve.

What I understood, although not well enough to explain at that age, was that my dad was not only a punisher and provider, but he also loved me. The rules were to keep me safe because he loved me.

Aren't God's rules really to protect us because he loves us?

Study questions:

Was that what God really wanted from Saul—a repentant heart—so that God could give him mercy and forgiveness?

Did the troubling spirit God sent allow Saul to reflect on his sins and repent?

Would an omniscient God know that Saul would not repent but seek relief?

Did God give the servants the wisdom to know David could provide Saul with relief?

Was this a blessing and training for David to be part of Saul's court?

Does trouble in our lives bring us into contact with people we would not otherwise meet?

Are God's rules for our protection because He loves us?

Is there possibly a purpose God has for changing our paths or circumstances?

Or do we have trouble because we brought it upon ourselves?

How can accepting God's love and forgiveness help you carry on?

8
FRIENDS, FOES, FAMILY AND GIANTS, OH MY!

SAUL HAS A problem. It is an evil spirit sent by God, and the evil spirit terrorizes him. Who correctly identifies the problem? A servant tells Saul it is an evil spirit.

Who tells Saul where the spirit came from? The same servant tells him the evil spirit was sent by God. What does the evil spirit do? The servant correctly says it is there to terrorize him.

What is the solution? Saul needs to listen to a skillful player on the harp, because when the musician plays, "You will be well." This is also correct.

How does a servant—not a wise man, not a priest—know exactly what is troubling Saul, as well as the solution?

It seems God not only sends the problem, but He also sends the solution.

Saul agrees to the plan. He tells his servants to bring a skillful musician to him. Another young man in Saul's presence knows a musician. He knows David, the son of Jesse, a Bethlehemite, who plays the harp and sings.

What a coincidence!

Not really; it is all part of God's plan, and the plan works. The evil spirit stops tormenting Saul, and his spirit is lifted when David plays his harp and sings.

Can singing praises to God lift our spirits today?

Saul loved David for providing relief and asked Jesse to allow David to stay with him.

Does David sing his own Psalms to Saul? David wrote Psalm 9.

> 1 I will give thanks to the Lord with all my heart; I will tell of Your wonders.
> 2 I will be glad and exult in You; I will sing praises to Your name, O Most High.
>
> —Psalm 9: 1,2

Does praising God irritate evil spirits enough that they leave?

—∿—

Because Saul likes David, he gives him an added job. Saul makes him his armor bearer. David learns about administration and weapons, and in addition, makes powerful contacts. These are skills and knowledge he could not obtain while shepherding.

David still goes home to tend sheep when he finishes his duties for Saul.

—∽∞—

During Saul's reign, the Philistines have constantly been at war with Israel. Saul has won multiple battles with God's guidance. But Saul does not have God's help now.

The Philistines have lined up for battle, and David is home, tending his sheep.

—∽∞—

For forty days, the Philistine giant, Goliath, challenges the Israelites to a one-on-one battle. The tall King Saul should have come forth.

But he does not; and he sends no one. He hides in his tent, exactly as he hid among the baggage on the first day of his reign.

> When Saul and all Israel heard these words of the Philistine, they were dismayed and greatly afraid.
> —1 Samuel 17:1

Saul's oldest son, Jonathan, in one battle with God's help had killed over two hundred Philistines.

However, he does not go to fight Goliath. Saul will not let Jonathan go. He is aware he placed a curse on Jonathan, and he fears he will see Jonathan die.

The battle lines are drawn, and no Israelite answers the challenge. Saul offers a reward to anyone who will fight Goliath. They will receive Saul's oldest daughter in marriage, and their father's home will be tax free.

David's three oldest brothers are among Saul's soldiers (Eliab, Abinadab, and Shammah). Jesse knows his sons are drawn up for battle, and he asks David to go to the battle lines to find out what is happening.

The next morning as David arrives at the battle lines, he greets his brothers, and he hears Goliath come and challenge the army of Israel.

> 4 Then a champion came out from the armies of the Philistines named Goliath, from Gath, whose height was six cubits and a span.
> 5 He had a bronze helmet on his head, and he was clothed with scale-armor which weighed five thousand shekels of bronze.
> 6 He also had bronze greaves on his legs and a bronze javelin slung between his shoulders.
> 7 The shaft of his spear was like a weaver's beam, and the head of his spear weighed six hundred shekels of iron; his shield-carrier also walked before him.
> 8 He stood and shouted to the ranks of Israel and said to them, "Why do you come out to draw up

in battle array? Am I not the Philistine and you servants of Saul? Choose a man for yourselves and let him come to me.

9 If he is able to fight with me and kill me, then we will become your servants; but if I prevail against him and kill him, then you shall become our servants and serve us."

10 Again the Philistine said, "I defy the ranks of Israel this day; give me a man that we may fight together."

—1 Samuel 4-10

Many of the men are fearful and run away.

David hears other men who remain talk about the reward that Saul is offering.

26 Then David spoke to the men who were standing by him, saying, "What will be done for the man who kills this Philistine and takes away the reproach from Israel? For who is this uncircumcised Philistine, that he should taunt the armies of the living God?"

27 The people answered him in accord with this word, saying, "Thus it will be done for the man who kills him."

28 Now Eliab his oldest brother heard when he spoke to the men; and Eliab's anger burned against David and he said, "Why have you come down? And with whom have you left those few sheep in the wilderness? I know your insolence and the wickedness of your heart; for you have come down in order to see the battle."

29 But David said "What have I done now? Was it not just a question?"

—1 Samuel 17: 26-30

David's words about fighting Goliath are told to Saul, and Saul sends for David.

32 David said to Saul, "Let no man's heart fail on account of him; your servant will go and fight with this Philistine,"

33 Then Saul said to David, "You are not able to go against this Philistine to fight with him; for you are but a youth while he has been a warrior from his youth."

34 But David said to Saul, "Your servant was tending his father's sheep when a lion or a bear came and took a lamb from the flock,

35 I went out after him and attacked him, and rescued it from his mouth; and when he rose up against me, I seized him by his beard and struck him and killed him.

36 Your servant has killed both the lion and the bear; and this uncircumcised Philistine will be like one of them, since he has taunted the armies of the living God."

37 And David said, "The Lord who delivered me from the paw of the lion and from the paw of the bear, He will deliver me from the hand of this Philistine."

—1 Samuel 17:32-37

David knows this feeling; he recognizes it as God's righteous anger. David knows he is to fight Goliath, and he knows he will win. He knows God is with him and will protect him.

—⟲—

Communication in their army is made by runners who carry written or verbal messages. Someone runs to tell Saul what David says. And the brothers' commander would have known that Saul had sent for David.

So, the commander sends his own runners to find out what is happening. Soon, he'll be informed that Saul is sending David to battle Goliath. And he learns that David carries only his shepherd's rod, his sling, and a few stones as weapons.

—⟲—

The commander seeks out David's brothers for information. He wants to learn more about David from these sons of Jesse. He surrounds them first with other soldiers and says, "Your brother David has volunteered, and Saul is sending him to fight Goliath."

Shammah tries to bolt, yelling, "No, stop him! He's just a boy!"

Immediately, Abinadab and Eliab stop their brother by tackling him. Shammah, who is now sobbing and trying to get away, looks up and bellows, "I love him; don't let him go!"

Eliab, the oldest, still holding Shammah down, looks up with resolve and says to the commander, "Send me in his place, sir. I will go."

Shammah, confused, twists around and looks at Eliab and says, "You don't even like him. Why would you do that?"

Eliab, although tearing up, screams at him, "Shut up! You are such an idiot!"

The commander shouts, "Not any of you are going! Get up! It's Saul's order to send David, and it's too late, anyway!"

The commander looks down the lines of soldiers, and then at Goliath, asking, "Does he have any chance? Any skills? He refused armor. He's taking only his shepherd's rod, a sling, and rocks."

Abinadab while dusting himself off, replies numbly, "He is a deadly shot with his sling, sir."

Shammah leaning now on his own rod adds, "Sir, he did kill a lion and a bear with his rod."

Eliab clears his throat and looks down.

The commander signals the other soldiers to surround them. "Don't let them go after their brother. And everyone, stand up, gird yourself, grab your weapons, and prepare for battle because the war is about to begin."

Then he rides off on his mule to take his own position.

Shammah says to his brothers, "Well, he did kill a lion and a bear with his own hands." Eliab doesn't reply; he continues staring off in the distance now.

Abinadab says, "Eliab thinks David just lied about that. He thinks David just found dead animals and claimed to have killed them."

Shammah shoves Eliab in the back and angrily replies, "Well, you don't know him then because David does not lie! Does it look like he is pretending to be brave?" He points to Goliath. "And he knows you don't like him, Eliab."

Eliab turns and stands up straighter, looks Shammah in the eye, and says, "You don't know everything. You don't know what it is like to be the oldest and responsible not only for myself but also for all seven of my brothers. You only see I get a double portion. Well, the responsibility is far more than double. If anything happens to David, will Father ask you why you didn't stop him? *No*! He will ask me. I would rather die than see that look on Father's or Mother's face. And do you think I would give my life for someone I don't love? You are a fool. I do love him. I love him like a father or protector—not like you. You love him like a pal or brother. There are things I don't like about him. I don't like his mouth, telling me what I should do. He has done that ever since he was a little boy, but I do love him!"

Shammah hangs his head, seeing Eliab in a different light, but adds, "You didn't understand why

David, when he was little, came to you shouting about the things the sheep needed. He looked up to you, and he loved the sheep. He thought you were the best person to help them. And he was aware you chose me to teach him how to be a shepherd. It hurt him knowing you would rather be with our nephews than with him."

Eliab doesn't answer. He considers Shammah's comments. His jaw muscles tighten and flex.

Abinadab, pointing at Goliath, says, "Well, maybe it was for this reason that Samuel picked him. Could it be that he is God's choice for this fight? I only hope and pray that God is with him."

Eliab straightens up, grabs his own weapons, and says, "Well, at any rate, we can't stop him, and we need to prepare for the battle. You two are to stay behind me. Do you understand? I'll not watch either of you die today! I will clear the path before you."

—◊◊◊—

Goliath makes no bones about it; he is an enemy to Israel. He wants to enslave them. He defies their God.

Saul is not about to fight; therefore, he relents and sends David. Saul offers two things—his own armor and a blessing. He asks for the Lord to be with David. If there was any doubt about Saul fighting in the battle, his offer to give up his armor left no doubt.

Saul is tall. When David puts on Saul's armor, he can hardly walk. David removes it, and kindly says he can't use the armor because he hasn't tested it.

David picks up his rod and five smooth stones. He places the stones in his pouch, and he holds the sling in his hand.

—๛—

Why five smooth stones? His bag was small, made to hold rocks for his sling or a small lunch. It would be like asking, "Why put six bullets in a six shooter?" Well, it doesn't hold seven. David knows he is going for a fight, and he is loading up with all he can.

David uses smooth rocks. We know the stitching on a baseball alters its flight. What would a knob on a rock do to its line of flight if hurled over 100 mph? A crack in the rock could make it split and go in two directions. Smooth rocks are needed to hold the flight direction and travel at maximum speed. Rocks in hand, David heads toward Goliath.

—๛—

David breaks through the ranks and starts down the hill toward the giant. The soldiers chant, "David, David!"

42 When the Philistine looked and saw David, he disdained him; for he was but a youth, and ruddy, with a handsome appearance.

43 The Philistine said to David, "Am I a dog, that you come to me with sticks?" And the Philistine cursed David by his gods.

44 The Philistine also said to David, "Come to me, and I will give your flesh to the birds of the sky and the beasts of the field."

45 Then David said to the Philistine, "You come to me with a sword, a spear, and a javelin, but I come to you in the name of the Lord of Hosts, the God of the armies of Israel, whom you have taunted.

46 This day the Lord will deliver you up into my hands, and I will strike you down and remove your head from you. And I will give the dead bodies of the army of the Philistines this day to the birds of the sky and the wild beasts of the earth, that all the earth may know that there is a God in Israel,

47 And that all this assembly may know that the Lord does not deliver by sword or by spear; for the battle is the Lord's and He will give you into our hands."

—1 Samuel 17:42-47

David places a rock into his sling and runs to meet Goliath.

His brothers watch David place the rock in the sling and they repeat the words they trained him with, "Smooth rocks, David. Smooth rocks for a dead aim."

Goliath's head, chest, arms, and legs are covered in armor. Only his face is open. David runs at him and slings the stone with all his might.

"Thunk! Crack!" He hears the sickening sound of flesh and bone breaking as the stone hits and sinks into Goliath's forehead.

"AACH!" Goliath's shield bearer screams and runs away.

Goliath's eyes roll back in his head. Blood gushes from the wound as he falls forward on his face. Billows of dust shoot up as the giant hits the dirt.

The Philistine army also scream in fear, drop their weapons, and run. Their belief in size, might, and weapons is demolished by the power of God. If this boy could do that, what will the Israeli soldiers do to them?

David runs to the body. Goliath is unconscious, but the increasing pool of blood shows life. Before Goliath can recover, David unsheathes Goliath's sword. He twirls it above his own head, and with a mighty swing, brings it down on Goliath's neck, severing Goliath's head from his body.

"To God be the Glory!" he shouts as he holds the bloody head by the hair and lifts it into the air.

His brothers all cheer, "He did it!" They slap each other on the back as well as the surrounding soldiers. Then they hoist their weapons, yell, and run to the battle.

The whole battle line of the Philistines is collapsing; they all run in fear. They are dropping armor, leaving tents, and abandoning equipment as they rapidly retreat. They cannot leave this valley soon enough. They are not fighting this army. They fear now that God empowers the Israelites.

Now the Israeli soldiers also feel empowered by God. They run after the Philistines, slaughtering any who are too slow to not outrun them. They are no longer afraid, because they are assured of their victory.

—◊◊◊—

God is capable of defending himself and his people; however, sometimes He chooses to work through people. He could have struck Goliath down without help. He chose to use David to bring Goliath down. God had been training David for this moment.

God uses miracles to open people's eyes to His glory and power and eminence over all. He uses people sometimes in the miracle, such as David, to give them recognition as one of God's chosen people.

The killing of an armored giant by a young man armed only with rocks was such a miracle that the story is still told today. It still gives glory to God and still brings fame to David.

—◊◊◊—

Goliath attacked God's people. He defied their God and wished to enslave them. What Goliaths do you see in your life? There is homelessness, poverty, wars, illiteracy, suffering, and slavery. Some things are attacks on people; some things are attacks on God.

The Bible says in Genesis:

In the beginning God created the heavens and the earth.
—Genesis 1:1

Is evolution an attack upon God? Even believers do not agree.

This is not my battle to fight. I am like Saul; I am really not prepared to do this battle. However, I know there are hundreds of scientists and scholars who believe in creation by God.

And they, like David, are throwing rocks ... and facts at evolution.

Rick McGough is one of them, and he has written several books. Here is a short quote, pointing out one problem with evolution. The fossil record does not support evolution. Transitional forms are an animal changing into a new kind of animal.

Rick McGough, author of Faith and Reason Made Simple, copyright 2018, page 174 states:

"Over 150 years of fossil discoveries since that time (time when Darwin's Origin of Species was written) have proven that the fossil record is void of transitional forms. If Darwin's theory were true, transitional fossils should be present by the millions. There are a few disputed samples of supposed transitional forms, such as the "archaeopteryx," which is supposedly a link between reptiles and birds, and "Lucy," which was supposedly a link between apes and humans. "Archaeopteryx" is now known to have been a bird and "Lucy" an ape. These are not transitional forms. In some instances, supposed transitional forms have actually been found to be frauds such as "Piltdown Man", probably the most famous fossil fraud ever, and the famous Triceratops dinosaur fossil at the National Museum of Natural History, Smithsonian Institution. The Triceratops fossil was eventually revealed to be of the bones of 14 different animals."

—⁓—

I believe in the Bible. If you think I am crazy or stupid for believing in creation by God, that's okay. I understand you have a right to your opinion. Let's be civil and agree to disagree, and then let's carry on.

—⁓—

Fight Your Fears

When fear is set before you,
And you stand with shaking feet.
From where will come your David
This Goliath to greet?

David lived and died among men,
And once was crowned a king.
Through him God sent a promise
To send an everlasting king.

Jesus is His name.
He lived and died and rose again.
If you need strength to face your fear,
Turn of course, to Him.

He always waits; He does not push.
And when you call on Him,
He comes with strength and righteousness;
And you can turn to Him.

So, learn the lesson David learned,
How to face your fears.
Get strength from the God of Glory.
He is here and He always hears.

David cannot save you,
He is no longer king.
Turn to the King of Glory,
Jesus, the Everlasting King.

Study questions:

Is it possible to love and hate your own family?

Does Eliab love David as family but does not like the things David says or does?

Is Eliab jealous that David was the one anointed?

Or does Eliab think David is less valuable because he is the youngest?

Who is Eliab's real foe—the real enemy?

Do you know what your Goliath is?

What makes the hair stand up on the back of your neck?

What makes you want to make a stand?

What makes you want to say:

- "No way, this is wrong!"
- "Absolutely, I agree with you!"
- "I'm in; what can I do to help?"

What is the spirit of God encouraging you to do?

PART III
RELATIONSHIPS WITH OTHERS

9
FRIENDS AND ENEMIES, AND ENEMIES WHO WERE FRIENDS

EVERYONE IS HAPPY in the Israel camp, right? No, not really.

Saul should be happy and relieved, but he is not. He now is suspicious. Saul has for a long time been trying to figure out the riddle: *Who is it God has chosen to be the next king?* Saul knows God has chosen someone to replace him.

Saul wonders, *How could this boy defeat Goliath?* Could it be God has chosen David to be the next king?

Saul then wonders about David and his family. Is David's father a leader; is he a warrior? What is David's family like?

Saul asks his commander, Abner, "Who is David's father?"

Abner answers, "I don't know much about the boy. I have only seen him come into your court and sing for you. He is from Bethlehem; I will find out more. He is obviously not a common boy. God's hand must be on him. Ask him when he returns and see what he has to say about his father."

Saul agrees.

When David returns, Saul asks him, "Who is your father?"

David replies, "Jesse, your servant from Bethlehem."

—⁓—

Later after receiving answers from his inquiry, Abner learns that it is true. Jesse is only a farmer from Bethlehem. He tells Saul.

Then Saul decides David is not a threat. The next king would not be the son of a farmer. David is a blessing to him. His singing drives the evil spirit away. Plus, David is very brave. Saul decides that David is to remain with him in the fortress. He tells Jesse he will no longer send David back.

Saul calls David to him. "David, I am no longer letting you return to your father to shepherd his sheep. You are too valuable to me. I will still have you sing, but I am also making you a captain over other soldiers. You are also a warrior."

After all, Saul did not know what to do with Goliath. David has saved him and Israel. Saul is pleased with David.

And David does not disappoint. In the future as a captain, he wins battle after battle for Saul.

—๛—

And how old is David when he kills Goliath?

David is probably sixteen or seventeen now. He has the strength, with his sling, to throw a rock with enough force to cave in Goliath's forehead. The frontal bone is very thick, and it would be even thicker on a giant. It would take a mighty blow to cave in the forehead.

—๛—

After David kills Goliath, Jonathan's heart goes out to David. When the battle is over, Jonathan greets him, "David, may God bless you, and I have a gift for you. In your next battles, you shall be armored."

And he hands David his armor and wraps his robe around David's shoulders. David starts to object.

"Jonathan, this is not right," David says.

But Jonathan insists. "No, David this is exactly right. I have liked you since I first heard you play your music for my father. But today, I see the man you are and the one you will become. You are worthy of armor, and you shall wear it. May there never be anything but honor between my house and yours."

This is Jonathan's pledge to David. He makes a covenant, a lasting agreement of allegiance to David. Jonathan will make three covenants with David—all promising his loyalty to David.

—⁓—

The Bible doesn't discuss it, but wouldn't David's brothers have come to congratulate him? Later, there seems to be healing in the family relations with Eliab. It may have begun here.

His brothers, as soldiers, pursue the Philistines in battle. But when the rout and chase are over, they seek out their little brother.

—⁓—

Shammah runs to David and gives him a big bear hug. He says, "Wow, it hurts to hug you with all that armor. Is that Jonathan's? You don't even look like my brother. You look like a prince!"

David laughs as he hugs all his brothers and says, "Yes, it's Jonathan's; he has gifted the armor to me, and Saul has ordered me into his service. I won't be returning to tend father's sheep." He gives Eliab a sideways glance.

Shammah adds, "I was so scared for you. I wanted them to stop you, and Eliab offered to take your place."

David now looks straight at Eliab, who only lowers his gaze.

David says, "I was scared for you three also, but I saw Eliab leading you, and I knew he was protecting you."

Eliab looks up at David but still does not speak to him. He turns and speaks to Shammah and Abinadab, "We are released from duty for now. Go home and tell Father and Mother we are all fine. And tell them about the battle and David. David and I need to talk."

After Shammah and Abinadab leave, Eliab walks over to David, and as he stands facing him, he says, "I have always passed you over, and you are a better man than I. You have grown up. Samuel did right to anoint you instead of me. And I am sorry. I have always disdained you because of that."

David looks into Eliab's eyes, smiles, and says, "I'm sorry I was such a brat too. I know when I was little, you didn't like it that I yelled at you and made Mother laugh."

Surprised and confused, Eliab shrugs and replies, "Well, Shammah said you yelled at me to help the sheep because I was the oldest, and you trusted me. He said you just wanted the sheep to be safe."

"Well, honestly, yes, maybe the first time. But I saw it irritated you, and I heard Mother laugh. So, other times, I was being a brat, as you called me. And I thought I was safe with Mother there, but I wasn't really safe. Was I?" David said with a bigger smile.

"What do you mean? I never laid a hand on you!" Eliab says, confused.

"No, you laid two. One to the seat of my pants, one to the scruff of my neck, and threw me in the wrestling match with Joab, Asahel, and Abishai. Joab had me down in a second, and they piled on." David laughs.

Eliab laughs now too. "Yeah, I did do that. And I was disappointed you got out shortly with some trick."

David nods. "Yeah, Shammah taught me that trick. Eliab, I'm sorry. You are the best big brother I could ever hope to have. Samuel couldn't anoint you because you already had a job protecting all of us. I only had sheep to protect, and someone else can do that. I knew you would be in front of Shammah and Abinadab, protecting them. Our family needs you, Eliab. I'm sorry for disrespecting you in the past. Let's put our childish things behind us and carry on with respect for each other from now on. You're the best big brother anyone could ever have!"

They shake hands, then hug. Eliab says, "Little brother has grown up. I am proud to be one of your brothers, David."

David looks up at Eliab and says, "You offered to go in my place? That's the kind of big brother everyone should have."

Eliab smiles. "And you really killed a lion and a bear? That wasn't a lie?"

They both laugh. And a new relationship is born between brothers.

—∞—

As time goes on, David serves Saul well as a captain; he wins every battle. He wins so many battles the women sing his praises, but the trouble starts when the women sing greater praises about David than Saul. Saul becomes jealous, angry, and suspicious again.

> 7 The women sang as they played, and said, "Saul has slain his thousands, and David his ten thousands."
> 8 Then Saul became very angry, for this saying displeased him; and he said, "They have ascribed to David ten thousands, but to me they have ascribed thousands. Now what more can he have but the kingdom?"
> 9 Saul looked at David with suspicion from that day on.
> —I Samuel 18:7-9

Although Saul is suspicious of David, his son, Jonathan, loves David as he loves himself.

David continues with his allegiance to Saul, although later Saul will try to kill him.

David's music is still the only solution for the evil spirit that troubles Saul. So, although David killed Goliath and he is a captain, he is still asked to play his harp for Saul.

Twice while David plays his harp for Saul, Saul hurls his spear at David. David escapes both times. And although Saul meant to kill him, he still is faithful to Saul.

Saul has become aware that the Lord is with David. He hates David for this and starts forming a plan to rid himself of David.

At first, Saul hopes the enemy will kill David. He has a plan.

Saul offers his oldest daughter in marriage if David fights valiantly. He makes David a commander over a thousand soldiers and sends him into a fierce battle.

David leads his men into battle and wins; he does not die. Saul is disappointed and gives his daughter to someone else.

David does not complain when Saul gives his oldest daughter in marriage to someone else. He feels he is inadequate to be the king's son-in-law, and he did not desire this daughter.

Later, Saul tries again with his younger daughter, Michal.

"David, you should be my son-in-law. You should marry Michal," Saul tells him.

"Saul, I am not worthy to be your son-in-law, and I have no dowry suitable for such a beautiful princess," David says.

Saul still wishes for David to die in battle, so he schemes. Saul has his servants convince David that he is worthy and that Saul desires him as a son-in-law. Michal is beautiful, and David is handsome. They find each other attractive, and they both desire this marriage.

So, when Saul offers David the opportunity to marry Michal again, he tells him, "David you are worthy, and I would like you to be my son-in-law. You are right—I should have a dowry suitable for a princess. I have money. I have land and flocks. I don't need more of them from you. I do have too many enemies, though, and if you kill one hundred Philistines, I would accept that as a suitable dowry for Michal."

David is pleased and Saul sends him to battle again. He sends David with a small band of soldiers, not the thousand. Saul expects the Philistines to kill him; however, David and his men kill two hundred Philistines.

This time, Saul keeps his promise. He gives Michal to David in marriage. She is highly spirited, and Saul hopes she will be a thorn in David's side, but David continues to prosper, and Saul's hatred, suspicion, and jealousy continues to grow.

Saul decides to get rid of David but not by his own hand. He orders his men to kill David. This time, Jonathan hears of it and talks Saul out of it.

Jonathan begs Saul, "Father, David is loyal to you. This would be an evil thing. You should not harm him. God will judge you. Please, do not do this! Rescind those orders for your own sake and our family."

Saul listens to Jonathan and withdraws the order.

However, as David continues to excel, Saul's hatred returns. David has God's blessing that Saul desires and once had. He hates seeing David blessed. Saul wants that blessing for himself.

When his hatred is at full bloom, Saul decides again to order David's death. This time, he keeps the plans from Jonathan. However, Michal learns of it and helps David escape.

Twice Saul's plan for David's demise is foiled by his own children.

When David escapes, he goes to Samuel in Ramah. David runs all night to tell Samuel all that Saul has done to him.

—ɯ—

Exhausted, David arrives in the morning. He is confused and runs to Samuel and falls at his feet, saying, "Samuel, may God be with you! May you have wisdom to speak to me!"

Samuel looks down upon David, who is dirty and disheveled. David is only a heap of a young man, lying at his feet. He remembers the shepherd boy with dirt on him, and the Lord saying, "This is the one; anoint him."

Because Samuel is a prophet, he knew there would be trouble and that David would be on his way to him. He looks at David with pity. He is still so young. He is also a fine young man. "Yes, Lord, you have picked a good one," Samuel whispers to God.

Samuel helps David up. "Let's get you some water, and yes, it is time I answer your questions. I will help you with all that is within my power."

David quickly cleanses himself and drinks some water. He apologizes for bursting in and then quickly begins telling Samuel all that is on his mind.

"I don't know what to do. I haven't done anything wrong, and yet, Saul is trying to kill me. He set the orders for his men to come to my home to kill me at this very dawn. There were guards all around my home. I had to climb out of my own window to escape. I ran all night to come here. It makes no sense! He gave his very own daughter, Michal, to me in marriage. He wanted me to be his son-in-law. I love her; I have been faithful to her. He made me a captain in his army, and I was also faithful then. I went out and won many battles for him. The Lord was with me, and we would win. And yet, while I played my harp for him, he has thrown his spear at me twice. I know he is bothered by an evil spirit, and I assumed it was the evil spirit who wanted me dead. I expected the mood would pass when he got his sanity back. But now, it seems, he wants me dead for no reason. Once before, he decided to order my death, and Jonathan talked him out of it. Will this pass too? What am I to do? Why does he love me and then hates me? He's the Lord's anointed; what am I to do? Can you speak to him for me?" David pleads.

Samuel, shaking his head, said, "I do not counsel Saul anymore. I have not since the day Saul ignored God's orders in the battle with King Agag. I prophesied that the kingdom was torn from him and given to another. It tore my heart too. I had been his counselor every step of the way. But he is not the same man God chose to be king. He has become proud and vain. He fights against God's will. We all struggle with God's will at times, but he chooses not to repent. It's his non-repentant spirit that draws the evil spirit. And God does not block it from him. He goes mad, and he has fits of rage, depression, suspicion, and pride. I see it in my mind. He knows God has chosen another to be king."

David looks up, and says, "Who?"

"You, David. God has chosen you. He told me to anoint you the next king, and I did." Samuel announces.

"What? I am no king! I am just a captain! And I was just a boy when you anointed me," David replies emphatically and inquisitively.

"Did you feel the spirit of the Lord come upon you when I anointed you? And has God's spirit been with you ever since? Has not God been training you to be king? Yes, for now you are a captain of soldiers. But someday, you will be a captain and a king for the people. As surely as you watched over and protected your sheep, someday you will watch over, protect, and lead God's people. God has chosen you, David. Saul knows it now. Don't you know it in your heart?" Samuel questions.

David, confused, answers, "When were you going to tell me?"

Samuel looks down. "I was going to tell you when God says to me, *'It is time, tell him.'* I see that time is now. If I had told anyone before, Saul would have killed us both, plus all your family. David let's go meet with the prophets and pray to God. See if God will confirm all that I have said to you and then ask God to guide you."

Then Samuel and David went to Naioth in Ramah, where all the prophets were prophesying. Both Samuel and David fell in the spirit and started prophesying too.

—⁓—

Meanwhile, back at the fortress, Saul is told his daughter has helped David escape. Saul is angry with Michal and sends for her.

Michal chooses to lie and says to her father, "I didn't want to help him! David threatened to kill me if I didn't go along with his plan."

Saul raises one eyebrow and observes her suspiciously. She starts twisting a little side to side, her eyes roll and dart around, trying not to look at him. She pulls her arms in front of her. He detects it all. Her tells show that she is lying.

Yes, he's seen this before. Years ago, this same little girl, swimming in her mother's clothing and sandals. Her mother asked Michal, "Are you wearing my clothing?"

Michal promptly answered, "No! Mine!" And all the time, swaying, eyes looking around, exactly as they are now. His little daughter, so adorable then ... not so much now.

He takes a deep breath and thinks it over in his head. *Yes, she is lying and probably everyone knows it. It is her devious talents that I thought would ensnare David, but maybe she still will be a snare for him. I will use her as bait. I will post spies to see if David returns or tries to contact her. I can't kill her. She's my daughter.*

He had hoped Michal's propensity for deceitfulness would upset and distract David. Then with his mind on her, instead of the battles, David would make mistakes that would cost him his life. However, that did not work.

Saul, feigning satisfaction with her answer, says, "Go home. I will protect you from him."

His mind continues to dwell on his children. *My own children turn away from me and pledge all their loyalty on David. Why can't they see? David is going to be the end of the house of Saul. He is my greatest enemy!*

He sends his men to hunt for David.

—⚹—

Later, some men return with the news that David is with Samuel at Naioth in Ramah.

"Go at once and kill him!" Saul shouts at his soldiers.

The soldiers obediently go to Naioth with the intent to kill David. However, when they arrive, the Spirit of God comes over them, and they fall, prophesying along with the prophets.

Saul doesn't hear back from them, as he expected. So, he sends messengers to find out what happened. They come back and report, "All your soldiers have all fallen under the spirit of God and are prophesying."

Saul is angry and immediately sends a second group of soldiers. These soldiers do not return, either. He again sends messengers to find out what is happening. They return telling him, "They did not kill David. They have also fallen under God's presence and are prophesying with the other soldiers."

Three times Saul sends soldiers to kill David, and three times the message comes back. "They have also fallen under God's presence and are prophesying instead."

"Ach! I see if I want something done, I must do it myself. Bring my armor! I will go and kill David myself!" Saul shouts.

When Saul arrives at Naioth, he also falls under the spirit of God. And Saul lies prophesying all day and night.

While Saul is prophesying, David returns to Saul's fortress and meets with Jonathan in secret. They renew the covenant between them.

David asks, "Jonathan, will you find out if Saul still wants to kill me? I hope that the prophecies will change his mind, and we can live peacefully again. Unless I know he accepts me again, I am afraid to face him."

Jonathan agrees and pledges his loyalty to David.

—〰—

When Saul returns, Jonathan talks to Saul. "Father, you know that David has always been faithful to you ..." And before he can finish—

"David must die, or you will never be king!" Saul yells at Jonathan and hurls his spear at him.

The prophecies have indeed opened Saul's eyes, and he hates what he knows. And he hates David even more.

Saul is intent upon killing David. He knows God has chosen David to be the next king. The kingdom is torn from him, and Jonathan will not be the next king. The riddle is solved. To Saul, David is his greatest enemy. David is the answer to the riddle, *Who has God named to be the next king?*

—m—

Jonathan secretly meets with David again. He tells him that Saul still intends to kill him. Jonathan is not jealous of David. He accepts that God has chosen David to be the next king. He renews his pledge, his covenant, to David. He tells David he must escape at once. David leaves immediately without weapons or supplies. Only four men go with him.

David has done nothing wrong, but he is persecuted by a madman—one who is the anointed king. This is like fighting another giant, except David chooses not to raise a hand against the anointed king. David runs for his life.

—m—

I remember a question on a quiz which I answered incorrectly.

The question was:

If a subject believes there is a burglar in the kitchen, is their level of anxiety higher if they are correct?

I answered yes, of course. The correct answer, though, is no. Their level of anxiety is based on their belief. They are equally afraid if they are wrong. They will soon be relieved when they find out they are wrong. But currently, their fear or anxiety is at the level it is because of their belief.

I have fled for my life, but maybe it was not necessary. I was in a relationship that was physically and mentally abusive: my first marriage. At times, my husband would snap, and he would be full of rage and suspicion. That is one of the reasons why I liked reading Samuel.

The first Bible books I completely read were I and II Samuel. I could relate to David being hated for no reason.

When I fled from my husband, I felt he would kill me if he could find me. Or if I stayed, he would kill me in a rage someday and then be very sorry because that was his pattern—rage, then remorse.

It did not matter if my beliefs were correct. I was living in a high level of anxiety and fear because of my experiences and my beliefs.

The scars or cracks I carried from that relationship were carried into other relationships.

I did not get advice from any pastor. I stayed away from church because I felt unworthy.

It would be twelve to thirteen years before I received advice from a pastor. That was the pastor who said God showed him a picture of me, and it was all cracked.

At this time, without advice, I ran first, and later, I jumped into other relationships.

I didn't need other relationships; I needed to heal.

My first husband obviously didn't kill me. But three years later, he did kill himself. I was right; he was capable of murder.

From all these experiences, I learned to carry on the best I knew how. I went to college, worked, and took care of my son.

Carry On

Although I am old and gray,
In me beats a heart
That was young one day.
In those days I remember—
Loving and losing,
And it all falling apart.

The dashing of my hope,
And the breaking of my heart.
The fear for my life,
And the fear of my death.
All too real—
All too real.

As I held your little hand in mine,
I knew God could hold me, too.
I knew I had to carry on,
Carry on, not just for me—
But also, for you.

Study questions:

Do you have enemies in your life?

Is there any way to make peace with them?

If you have opposition, would God prefer you to fight or take flight?

Besides prayer, how do we know what to do?

Can trouble come to us if we have done nothing wrong?

Have you ever had to flee from trouble?

10
RUNNING AND HIDING

MAYBE YOU HAVEN'T had an angry king seeking
your life, but have you ever dealt with a bully or
mean neighbor? Maybe you have had a classmate
or coworker who dislikes you for no reason or a
spouse, teacher, or boss who is always putting you
down.

The number of people job-hopping, church-hop-
ping, and getting divorces is on the rise. I think
most people can relate to having someone in their
life who takes offense for no reason or overreacts
to a disagreement. Can you relate to someone who
finds offense in something that was not meant to
be an insult?

—∿—

Although David remains true, Saul's level of resentment only continues to increase until it reaches the breaking point. At that point, Saul can be happy only if David is dead.

David must now flee for his life. He runs, without weapons or food. He has four trustworthy men with him. The Bible does not say who is with him. It does say that when he stops at Nob, the priest asks David about the young men with him.

Jonathan sees that not only David's life is in jeopardy but also David's family. If Saul can't kill David, he might take it out on David's family. Jonathan knows David must run for his life. He sends for David's brothers and his nephews to warn them; they must escape also.

After Jonathan's warning, his brothers Eliab and Abinadab go to Bethlehem to gather and warn the family. Shammah, Joab, Abishai, and Asahel go with David.

David runs to Nob and asks for five loaves of bread. The high priest at Nob gives David and the young men five loaves of bread and the sword of Goliath. The priest does not know David is running from Saul.

When Saul hears of David's escape to Nob, he becomes crazy with anger. Saul orders all the priests from Nob and their families, including women and children—even their livestock to be slaughtered—all because the priest has given David five loaves of bread and Goliath's sword.

David leaves Nob and flees to Gath, the Philistine city Goliath came from. David thinks it is safe there because Saul will not go into an enemy city; however, David is recognized. Someone names him as one of Saul's warriors—the one who killed Goliath of Gath.

(*Not all David's decisions were good ones.*)

The Philistines capture him and bring him before the king. It is then that David feigns madness. He slobbers, yells, and scratches at the door. He is so good at acting crazy that King Achish says, "Remove him from my sight!"

As soon as he is released, David runs from Gath to the caves of Adullam.

David has gone from being a son-in-law to the king and a captain to a fugitive. In the recent past, he ran into battle and won, but now he is running for his life. He fears for himself and his family. This may be the lowest he has felt in his life.

—m—

David writes a Psalm to God from a cave. When he arrives at Adullam, as he is fleeing from Saul, he tells his troubles to God.

1 I cry aloud with my voice to the Lord; I make supplication with my voice to the Lord.

2 I pour out my complaint before Him; I declare my trouble before Him.

3 When my spirit was overwhelmed within me, You knew my path in the way where I walk they have hidden a trap for me.

4 Look to the right and see; for there is no one who regards me; there is no escape for me; no one cares for my soul.

5 I cried out to You, O Lord; I said, "You are my refuge, my portion in the land of the living.

6 Give heed to my cry, for I am brought very low; deliver me from my persecutors, for they are too strong for me.

7 Bring my soul out of prison, so that I may give thanks to Your name; the righteous will surround me, for You will deal bountifully with me."

—Psalm 142

David, a man after God's own heart, feels close enough to God to share his pain and ask for help.

The cave of Adullam will later be referred to as *David's stronghold* because it is not long before God sends help, and David is no longer alone.

—⚒—

At Adullam, all his brothers, family, and their households come to him. In addition, all discontented people flock to him. Soon, David has 400 men willing to serve and follow him.

David's parents are old now, but they are with him at the caves. Later, he finds a better place for them. He takes his mother and father to Mizpah in Moab. He asks permission of the king of Mizpah to leave them there until he returns for them. They will remain at Mizpah while David is in the stronghold.

I note the Bible says *all* his brothers came. There is no mention of Eliab criticizing David this time. He must have come to terms with David receiving God's anointing.

In addition to family and soldiers, God also sends a spiritual advisor. Abiathar, the high priest's son, is the only person to escape the slaughter at Nob. He has come to David for protection. He has brought the high priest's ephod with him.

An ephod is the linen garment worn by the priests. However, the high priest's ephod also has a breastplate with precious stones. And the stones have the ability to give answers from God: yes and no, or *Urim* and *Thummim.*

Because of the great evil Saul has done to the priests at Nob, David now has a spiritual advisor and the high priest's ephod. David uses the ephod many times to find God's direction.

For months and even years, Saul continues to hunt for David. And David continues to move about the country, trying to stay hidden from Saul.

During these hunts, twice Saul is delivered into David's hands. Both times David refuses to hurt or kill Saul. David confronts Saul with evidence that he could have killed him. Both times, Saul relents and retreats.

David spends years in exile, running and hiding, yet he remains faithful to God. Many of his Psalms are written to God, pleading for help. However, he always gives glory to God somewhere in his Psalm.

1 Contend, O Lord, with those who contend with me; fight against those who fight against me.

2 Take hold of buckler and shield and rise up for my help.

3 Draw also the spear and the battle-axe to meet those who pursue me; say to my soul, "I am your salvation."

4 Let those be ashamed and dishonored who seek my life; let those be turned back and humiliated who devise evil against me.

5 Let them be like chaff before the wind, with the angel of the Lord driving them on.

6 Let their way be dark and slippery, with the angel of the Lord pursuing them.

7 For without cause they hid their net for me; without cause they dug a pit for my soul.

8 Let destruction come upon him unawares, and let the net which he hid catch himself; into that very destruction let him fall.

And my soul shall rejoice in the Lord; it shall exult in His salvation.

10 All my bones will say, "Lord, who is like You, who delivers the afflicted from him who is too strong for him, and the afflicted and the needy from him who robs him?"

11 Malicious witnesses rise up; they ask me of things that I do not know.

12 They repay me evil for good, to the bereavement of my soul.

13 But as for me, when they were sick, my clothing was sackcloth;

I humbled my soul with fasting, and my prayer kept returning to my bosom.

14 I went about as though it were my friend or brother; I bowed down mourning, as one who sorrows for a mother.

15 But at my stumbling they rejoiced and gathered themselves together; the smiters whom I did not know gathered together against me, they slandered me without ceasing.

16 Like godless jesters at a feast, they gnashed at me with their teeth.

17 Lord, how long will You look on? Rescue my soul from their ravages, my only life from the lions.

18 I will give you thanks in the great congregation; I will praise You among a mighty throng.

19 Do not let those who are wrongfully my enemies rejoice over me; nor let those who hate me without cause wink maliciously.

20 For they do not speak peace, but they devise deceitful words against those who are quiet in the land.

They opened their mouth wide against me; they said, "Aha, aha, our eyes have seen it!"

22 You have seen it, O Lord, do not keep silent; O Lord, do not be far from me.

23 Stir up Yourself, and awake to my right and to my cause, my God and my Lord.

24 Judge me, O Lord, my God, according to Your righteousness, and do not let them rejoice over me.

25 Do not let them say in their heart, "Aha, our desire!" Do not let them say, "We have swallowed him up!"

26 Let those be ashamed and humiliated altogether who rejoice at my distress; let those be clothed with shame and dishonor who magnify themselves over me.

27 Let them shout for joy and rejoice, who favor my vindication; and let them say continually, "The Lord be magnified, who delights in the prosperity of His servant."

28 And my tongue shall declare Your righteousness and Your praise all day long.

—Psalm 35

David in his misery prays to God for deliverance. God hears his prayer, and David thanks God. David declares God's righteousness and praises him all day long. David continues to thank God, even though Saul still pursues him. No place is safe long. David must continue moving about.

As he moves about the country, David gathers new alliances—and wives. Saul's daughter Michal has been given in marriage to another man. So, she is not with him.

David marries his second wife from Jezreel, Ahinoam.

Later, he marries Abigail, Nabal's widow from Carmel. Nabal was a wealthy man who had large herds and many servants. David has control of Nabal's wealth now.

―∿―

Have you ever been in a situation where you don't know what to do? I have more times than I can count. It's daily, in fact. I can think of so many things to do that I am not sure where to start.

I began this book years ago, and then set it aside for years. I really didn't know how to proceed. I felt confused, and I had no direction. I got sidetracked with household chores and family matters.

I start trying to sort out household items we no longer need but still have. I cannot decide what should be kept, what should go. And should it be thrown away or given away? Is it valuable? Who would know? Who might want it?

What about money matters—should I get another job?

How can I spend less or earn more?

Should we stay here?

Should we move?

What about family or friends; should I travel to see those far away? When should I go? Whom should I see?

I have found that sitting and questioning is not the answer. I must do something, even if it is wrong. God can't guide me if I sit like a rock, staring at the TV or out the window.

Here's an example of what I mean: I asked my one-year-old great-granddaughter to bring me the red ball. She brought a green ball to me. I'd tell her, "No, not that one."

She'd return it and try again.

"No, the red one, not the blue one."

She did not know colors yet. She would continue until she brought the red one and then we both cheered. By telling her, she began to see the difference between red, blue, and green. I'm thankful she is not color blind. And no, I didn't need the red ball; I was trying to teach her something.

God cares much more for us than I do for my children or grandchildren, as precious as they are. I found that if I listen, He is always trying to teach me something, even if it's "No, not that."

I'm trying to learn how to hear God's voice. It is a lifelong process.

At a low point in my life, I wrote my psalm to God:

To the God of Life

Dearest God,

You are the God of Life,
And though I am not dead,
The Joy of Life is gone—
And I am filled with dread.

I need a Guide, a Savior,
To pull me from this pit.
The burden of my debt
Makes me feel unfit.

These burdens all surround me
And press upon my mind.
The answer is beyond me;
I search but cannot find.

I need some help,
A coach, a hand,
I need—
The beginning of a plan.

Please Lord,
Hear my prayer—
And bring Life
To me again.

Study questions

When we need change, what should we do?

With whom should we go?

Where do we find alliances?

With what groups should we join or associate?

How do we find out what we are called to do?

Where should we go when we feel it's time to leave?

11
DAVID—TAKING CHARGE OF HIS TRIBE

YOU MIGHT THINK David is a victim, but he isn't really. He is falsely accused and pursued, but he is not stuck in self-pity, remorse, depression, or denial, as so many people with victim mentality seem to be. All those feelings lead to hopelessness, which leads to inaction. Victims feel powerless to change. Action requires hope and confidence that things can change.

David doesn't like the position he finds himself in, but he is solving the problem. He is trying to carry on. He is a man of action.

Victors see a problem, look for a solution, and act. If the first plan doesn't work—like going to Gath—victors turn to plan two. Examples of plan two would be feigning insanity to escape. Then plan three is to run to a cave and hide in it.

David then tries his best plan, his next plan—ask God for help.

3 For a dream comes through much effort.
—Ecclesiastes 5:3

In Chapter 10, you read David's Psalm 142. You can see depression or fear in that passage. But David states the problem to God, and he asks for help.

Below in Psalm 145, you can see David thanking and blessing God for his goodness. He does not forget to thank God for answering his prayers.

1 I will extol You, my God, O King, and I will bless Your name forever and ever.
2 Every day I will bless You, and I will praise Your name forever and ever.
3 Great is the Lord, and highly to be praised, and His greatness is unsearchable.
4 One generation shall praise Your works to another, and shall declare Your mighty acts.
5 On the glorious splendor of Your majesty and on Your wonderful works, I will meditate.
6 Men shall speak of the power of Your awesome acts, and I will tell of Your greatness.
7 They shall eagerly utter the memory of Your abundant goodness and will shout joyfully of Your righteousness.
8 The Lord is gracious and merciful; and slow to anger and great in loving kindness.

9 The Lord is good to all, and His mercies are over all His works.

10 All Your works shall give thanks to You, O Lord, and Your godly ones shall bless You.

11 They shall speak of the glory of Your kingdom and talk of Your power;

12 To make known to the sons of men Your mighty acts and the glory of the majesty of Your kingdom.

13 Your kingdom is an everlasting kingdom, and Your dominion endures throughout all generations.

14 The Lord sustains all who fall and raises up all who are bowed down.

15 The eyes of all look to You, and You give them their food in due time.

16 You open Your hand and satisfy the desire of every living thing.

17 The Lord is righteous in all His ways and kind in all His deeds.

18 The Lord is near to all who call upon Him, to all who call upon Him in truth.

19 He will fulfill the desire of those who fear Him; He will also hear their cry and will save them.

20 The Lord keeps all who love Him, but all the wicked He will destroy.

21 My mouth will speak the praise of the Lord, and all flesh will bless His holy name forever and ever.

—Psalm 145

—〜—

David now knows he has been anointed to be the next king. He has clarity.

And having clarity, he now adds action.

He first sets up a strong inner circle. He calls his brothers and nephews together at Adullam to set the groundwork.

The Bible frequently mentions his nephews. The three sons of his sister, Zeruiah, were Abishai, Joab, and Asahel. He has another nephew, Amasa, son of his other sister, Abigail. Amasa is mentioned more in II Samuel; he may have been several years younger than the other nephews.

David sends Asahel to round up his brothers, nephews, and loyal soldiers who have followed him here to Adullam.

David has a group of staunch soldiers who are called David's Mighty Men. There are as many as thirty-seven in this group. Abishai, his nephew, is their captain. Asahel, another nephew, is listed among them.

Joab is the commander of his army.

—〜—

David speaks clearly and with authority. "I didn't bring you here, but you are all here because of me. Let me be clear; your life is in danger if you stay with me. Anyone who wishes to go, must go beyond Judah and Israel because King Saul has declared me an enemy. He seeks my life and any that are found with me. If you stay with me, know this: I am in control here. My family knows that Samuel anointed me as a boy. I am telling you now, he anointed me to be the next king. God has been preparing me to lead Judah and Israel ever since. My training began from learning to guard sheep, to fighting Goliath, to commanding soldiers for Saul. It has all been part of my training to be the next king. I accept this now. If you cannot, then you should depart from me. I know we are outnumbered. Only with God do we have a chance. If God intends for me to be king, he will protect me. Saul has been king many years and accomplished many great things; he is God's anointed king for now. I will not harm him. I will not tolerate any of you trying to harm him or his sons. We will let God determine the days of Saul's life. I need to surround myself with those I trust—those who believe in me. Who can accept what I have said? Who will live and fight with me?"

David's top thirty, his Mighty Men, his nephews, and others shout, "We will pledge our loyalty and fight for you!"

—⁓—

Afterward, Joab asks to speak privately with David.

Joab looks sharply into David's eyes and says, "David, you know that war can be messy. It is kill or be killed. I will continue to fight for you and protect you. But if I see my life or your life in danger, I must have the right to take that life, whether it is King Saul or anyone else. Promise me you will not kill me or order my death for killing those I believe to be a danger, regardless of who that might be. Promise me, and I will lead your troops as I have. I will protect you and your kingdom. You have to trust me too. Do you promise?"

David feels this is a mutual trust and agrees.

David will rue many of Joab's decisions. Joab will take many lives that David would have spared. However, David never orders Joab's execution. Joab, his nephew, will remain the commander of David's army.

—⁂—

After months of hiding in the wilderness and moving constantly, David's tribe continues to grow until he has 600 men and their families.

David seeks a place to stay. Traveling and hiding is hard for the families. He returns to Gath, the same Philistine city where he feigned insanity to escape. He believes Saul will not go there, and he has a plan to trick King Achish into letting them stay this time.

David pretends to be an enemy to Israel. His men raid cities and bring back plunder for themselves and King Achish. David always tells the king it is from a raid on a city in Israel, but that is never true. They are raiding cities far from them who are enemies to Israel.

King Achish of Gath thinks David is his servant. When David sees the king trusts him, he asks for his own city outside of Gath. Achish gives David, his men, and their families the southern Philistine city of Ziklag. David and his men stay in Ziklag fourteen months.

After fourteen months, Achish asks David and his men to go to the battle with him. The Philistines are going to war against Saul in the northern part of Israel. David and his men travel with Achish. However, the other Philistine leaders do not trust David, so Achish sends David and his men back to Ziklag.

When they return to Ziklag, they see that it has been raided. All their wives and children are missing.

At this point, David's men are ready to stone him and leave.

David inquires of God with the ephod. The answers he receives tells him that their families are alive and that he and his men can save them from the raiders.

The men are already tired from the long trip back to Ziklag. Nevertheless, they pursue the raiders and recapture their families. No family members are lost, as God had promised.

David takes pity on the men who are too exhausted to make it all the way to recapture their families. He insists that they share in the spoils also. This sets a precedent that *those with the baggage share equally with those on the front lines.*

David solves the problem, gets answers from God, encourages and leads his men.

—〰—

The Philistines win the battle with Saul. Saul and Jonathan are killed in the battle. Saul's son Ish-bosheth is crowned king of Israel. This is the northern kingdom of Israel.

—〰—

David and his men are not happy about living in a Philistine city of Ziklag. Again, David inquires of God, using the ephod, and is told to move to Hebron in Judah.

When David goes to Hebron, the people of Judah come and crown him to be their king.

David is the King of Judah. It is known as the southern kingdom. He will be king in Hebron for seven and a half years.

—〰—

Believe me, writing this book was a dream I have had for years, but I only got started and never carried on. I was blocked by I am not good enough. I never was good at English grammar. No one will listen. I am nothing.

When I stopped calling myself names and started this book, I found out that, yes, it is a lot of work! I have managed to delete several pages with an errant touch. I have asked friends and family to read and make suggestions. Most of them could not find the time. Where is all this time going? It seems to be always lost. Others said they could not open the link but did not tell me until much later.

Thank you very much for my few beta readers and supporters!

But the problem was mine; it was not their problem. To be the victor, I had to take on the problem and solve it and put the solution into action.

Problems I solved—

- *I needed to be clear about "Who am I?" I am an author.*

- *I needed confidence in "What can I do?" I can write a book.*

- *I had to take control and do the work. I can be my own boss.*

My dream is that this book will be a blessing to many. I am doing the activity. I am solving the problems. I am doing the work.

My dream does require much effort. With God's help, I am up for the task. God helps me to carry on.

Study questions:

Make your choice: are you a victim or a victor?

If you have problems, what can you do to solve them?

What is your dream?

Do you believe God will help you achieve your dreams?

Are your dreams in alignment with God's goals for your life?

Is your dream worth working out the problems and dedicating the time and effort?

If you decide it is, then you must carry on.

12
GUARD YOUR HEART

I HAD A dream that I was driving my car, and my friend was ahead of me in her car. We were both going to see Jesus. We were traveling in my hometown, driving down the main street. My friend did not see Jesus, who was standing on the far side of an empty parking lot. So, she kept driving, getting farther and farther away from him.

I turned right, toward Jesus, and what was a parking lot suddenly became full of cracks and broken concrete piled up, like an earthquake had moved the ground. My car was stuck on a concrete chunk. I was close to Jesus, but I couldn't move. In my dream, I had to arrive in my car, and now the wheels were not on the ground.

I could see my friend driving down the easy road but heading out of town. The path was smooth but away from Jesus. My friend was enjoying the drive, singing along the way, never noticing I was stuck, or that the easy road didn't lead to Jesus.

In my dream, I finally realized I could not help my friend. And my friend could not help me. I was stuck because of my choices. I really had known this was not a road or parking lot. Why did I turn here? The only one who could help me was Jesus.

When I asked Jesus for help, he told me I was stuck because I had tried a short cut. This was not the path he had prepared for me. He said I would be stuck for a while, but later, he would help me.

—m—

Guard Your Heart

Guard your heart,
Although you cannot see,
Your heart will choose
The path of your destiny.

Guard your heart,
For you cannot tell,
Who will lead you right
Or who will lead you to evil.

Guard your heart,
For your heart will lead
You toward God,
Or away from Thee.

Guard your heart,
So that you will see,
The good path placed before you,
That leads to your safe destiny.

For David, there is a long time of running and hiding. During this time, he has to make new plans and develop new alliances. He must solve problems, such as when his men all want to stone him and leave.

It takes many years, but David continues to carry on. He is finally crowned king. He is not king over all Israel, not yet, but he is king over Judah. He is a victor.

—ɯ—

Now as king, David has the power to give gifts. David requests to speak to Shammah privately. His brother is a little concerned and wonders if he has done something wrong.

Shammah nervously enters, kneels, and with his right arm crossed over his heart, he says, "My king!"

David sees Shammah's shaking. He does not mean to make Shammah feel subservient. David helps him to stand. "Shammah, stand up. We are brothers; call me David when we are alone. I called you here as a brother to thank you. And secondly, as a king, to do something for you."

"Okay, David, but you are also my king. It's nerve-wracking to be called before one's king, even if he is your brother," replies Shammah while still shaking.

"Shammah, I want to thank you for how you treated me as a child. And how well you taught me to lead the sheep." David smiles and adds, "… and how to sling rocks—that was kind of important."

They both laugh.

Shammah adds, "Yes, I remember one shot going backward and one hitting me on the foot." He lifts one foot as if it is still sore.

"Yes, and again, please accept my most humble apology about that," David says as he jokingly places his left hand over his heart and nods his head in acquiescence.

They both laugh and now Shammah feels less tense.

David continues, "At one time, I didn't think I could ever sling a rock and hit anything. You were patient and encouraged me. So, I kept practicing, and I did learn. And later in life, when I was fleeing from King Saul, you ran with me to Nob. And you stayed with me as I ran to Gath, and from there, to the cave of Adullam. You have been with me in every step and every battle since we left Saul. Shammah, you are famous. Do you know it?"

Shammah laughs and says, "I don't think I'm famous; you are. I'm just a brother to the king and one of your soldiers."

"No, Shammah, you are famous. And your name meaning *destruction* does not fit you. As your king, I am renaming you Shimeah (meaning fame), that is, if you are willing to receive it."

Shammah cannot believe it; he has always hated his name. Although when he was in battle, he felt he would bring destruction on his enemies. Fame, a new name for him? He realizes he hasn't even answered, as he was so busy imagining it.

"Oh, yes, yes! I would love it changed; thank you, David," he exclaims.

"Good. We will do it publicly, so forevermore in the stories, you will be called Shimeah because you are famous," David replies as he slaps Shimeah on the back.

—⁓—

David is king over Judah, and he surrounds himself with his Mighty Men (his top thirty warriors). A few names are prominent in David's future. One name on the list of David's Mighty Men is Uriah the Hittite. Another important name is Ammiel (also called Eliam). He is the son of Ahithophel, a counselor to Saul. Ammiel is the father of Bathsheba.

The Mighty Men are comparable to our Special Forces. They are David's top soldiers and his guard. The captain of David's guard, Benaiah, is one of his Mighty Men.

In a group of thirty, there would be smaller sets—men who know each other and are trained to work as a unit. Uriah knows Bathsheba's father well. All the Mighty Men are all friends. It's a tight group.

—◇—

This is the story of Bathsheba, also called Bathshua.

Years ago, when Saul first made David a captain, Ammiel was one of his top soldiers. Ammiel was loyal to David. Though, when David fled from Saul into the wilderness, he could not join him. He had his wife and one daughter, Bathsheba, to protect.

However, when David was given the city of Ziklag, Ammiel rejoined with him there. He left his wife and daughter with his father, Ahithophel.

—◇—

Ahithophel is a counselor to Saul. Saul questions Ahithophel about Ammiel going to David's camp. But Ahithophel is shrewd.

Explaining to Saul, Ahithophel says, "Well Saul, you let David go twice. You decided he was not a threat. And you know David with his few bands of men is not going to attack you. Besides, if there is something to report, don't you think I will find out from my son? And I will report it to you at once. It's a good thing to have ears in David's camp."

That convinces Saul, and he does not interfere.

Then as now, wars were not the only way people died. Ahithophel's wife and Bathsheba's mother die of illnesses. Bathsheba is his only grandchild, and Ahithophel is very protective of her. He stays a counselor to Saul until Saul dies in battle.

After Saul's and Jonathan's deaths, another of Saul's sons, Ish-bosheth, is crowned king over Israel. Ahithophel sees David will be the more prosperous king. He furtively goes to David's camp with Bathsheba.

David had already been crowned King of Judah and moved to Hebron.

Ahithophel comes to be a counselor now to David. He will also join his son, Ammiel, who is one of David's Mighty Men. Bathsheba travels with her grandfather and is glad to be reunited with her father. She is probably five or six years old now.

The city of Hebron is safer for the families, but the men still face wars. Now they are battling the Israelites as well as the Philistines.

David has thousands of men now, but he knows his Mighty Men by name. The captain of the Mighty Men, Abishai, is another of David's nephews. Benaiah, another Mighty Man, is captain of his guard. These men surround David in battle and in peace. His Mighty Men are always with him.

—⁜—

When David and the Mighty Men return from battle, they see Ahithophel and Bathsheba watching for them—two small figures peering out, standing high on a hill to get the best view. They eagerly look for Ammiel.

As they draw closer, Bathsheba works her way down the hill. She jumps up and down with excitement. When they draw close enough, Ahithophel lets her loose.

She comes running.

"Daddy, Daddy!" she shouts as she jumps into Ammiel's arms.

Ammiel laughs and swings her around in his arms. "What have you been up to? Did you miss me?" he asks.

"I did, I did miss you so. I haven't had a hug in weeks!" she says. Her grandfather is not the hugging type.

David watches and laughs. He has a daughter now too. He wonders if his daughter will ever be that glad to see him.

Bathsheba and her dad walk hand-in-hand back to the compound. She always has a lot of questions—things she has been thinking about while he was away.

"Daddy, do you think you will ever get another wife?" she quizzes.

"No, I never plan to do that," he replies.

"Why? David has a lot of wives," she questions.

"Yes, I know he does, but I had one great love. Your mom was the love of my life. That is enough for me. I miss her. But I see her in your eyes. And I always have her here in my heart. She is with me always," he says as tears come to his eyes.

He ticks her cheek, smiles, and adds, "And I will love you, always! That is enough for me."

Ahithophel is proud of Ammiel; he is a great warrior—one of David's Mighty Men. He expects Ammiel to always return. For a long time, he is right.

—⁂—

About four years later, at Hebron, the men are again at battle.

During this battle, while sword fighting, Ammiel is struck by an arrow. It cuts him on the right side of his neck. Blood spurts everywhere. He bests his combatant with a quick sword thrust, but he immediately collapses.

The Mighty Men circle around him. Uriah checks his wound and tries to stop the bleeding. Ammiel's eyes stare at nothing; he grabs Uriah's beard and says, "Take care of Bathsheba." These were his last words as he dies in Uriah's arms.

—⁂—

After the battle is over, Ammiel's body is carried home on his shield. David walks with his body, honoring Ammiel.

High on the hill, two figures see it in anguish.

Ahithophel bellows, "AHH!"

Bathsheba screams, "No, not my Daddy!"

She is too quick for Ahithophel; she runs down the hill. She is too tricky for the soldiers, who try to stop her. She dodges them and runs past.

David, trying to shield her from the trauma of seeing Ammiel's bloody, lifeless body, opens his arms wide. She tries to dodge him too, but he side-steps. She runs full into him.

She buries her face in David's chest, and the sadness within her explodes. She sobs uncontrollably now. Her tears flow freely. "No, no, not my Daddy!"

Her sadness brings tears to David's eyes. He softly tells her, "I will miss him too. Your father was a great warrior; he was one of my Mighty Men. Please, let us make him presentable; he wouldn't want you to see him like this. Come now, let's go back together."

He looks for Ahithophel but cannot spot him.

In his grief and anger, Ahithophel has walked away. David wonders why he isn't there to comfort Bathsheba.

David gives Bathsheba the hug that she is missing, and they walk back together.

—⟋⟍—

Time has passed: they all have had to carry on in their own way.

While David is king in Judah, six sons are born, one to each of his six wives.

Bathsheba is growing into a young lady.

Ahithophel stays a counselor to David, even though his son has died in battle.

Ahithophel supervises Bathsheba as though she is one of his business ventures. He's a businessman and a counselor. He is not a hugger like her father, but he cares for her. He often takes her with him to impart proper guidelines of behavior.

She is about eleven or twelve years old now, and one day, he takes her with him as he counsels with David. He has two goals on the agenda for her today. One, she should learn the protocol on how to approach a king. And two, to make sure David recognizes Bathsheba, the daughter of Ammiel, who died fighting for him. Ahithophel thinks, *Yes, David owes us both; he should be reminded.*

All during their talk, Bathsheba stares at David. She follows his every movement and word. She remembers the aroma of his chest, the tenderness of his hug. She is quiet, as trained, until she leaves with her grandfather.

"David is so handsome; I'm going to marry him someday! You could arrange it, Grandfather," she exclaims.

"No, you are not! And no, I will not!" Ahithophel replies emphatically.

Confused, Bathsheba stares at him. She thinks he should want her to be a queen. He is always talking about prestige.

Ahithophel scowls, turns, and points to her, saying, "Hmph! He has six wives already and seven if you count Michal. And he's attempting to get her here. Who knows how many wives he will have by the time he is old? I will not have you be number ... number ... oh, whatever number! You are too important. You will have an important husband, one who cares for you. You will be wife number one, and the only wife. Your father, rest his soul, asked Uriah to watch over you. He is one of David's Mighty Men, as was your father. I think Uriah would make a fine husband for you."

He turns from her, scowls even harder, and adds half under his breath, "Besides, it's because of David your father is dead." He doesn't say it, but he thinks, *and I hate him for that.*

She knows better than to argue with her grandfather, but to herself, she thinks, *Father loved serving David, and he died well and honorably. And besides, Uriah is okay. He's thoughtful. He remembers my birthday and brings gifts. But he's no David. I can't see Uriah being my one great love.*

She remembers what her father said about having one great love. David has many wives, but he doesn't seem to be in love. The wives are all puffed up about their sons and parade them around like prizes. She notes they all have only one son. David must not be in love with his wives, or he would not need so many. She knows she loves David, and she begins to picture him loving her too. They would be happy and have many sons.

—∿—

David's tribe is a close group made up of family and followers. They are at war with Israel, and they stay close together. The children play together, and someone is always assigned to watch over them.

Bathsheba is one of the older children now, and she sometimes must watch over them. When her grandfather is not around, she claims her David to the rocks, trees, and small children.

Shimeah, his brother, previously known as Shammah, sends word for David to talk to him in private at his home.

Shimeah's sons, Jonadab and Jonathan, are with him. His children often play together with David's sons. Jonadab is friends with David's son, Amnon. They are about four or five years old.

As David enters their home, Shimeah's boys shout with glee, "Uncle David! Hug me first! Hug me first!"

They run for their hugs.

David laughs, holds out his arms, and says, "Well, I came to talk to your father, but I always have time for hugs."

The boys almost knock him over, as they hit him at the same time.

Shimeah says, "Hey, Jonadab, ask Uncle David about your number one question."

Jonadab says, "Is Bathsheba your number one?"

David, confused, says, "My number one what?"

Jonadab says, "Your number one queen. She tells us that all the time."

David, trying to brush this off, says, "Oh, she's just playing. And she's too young to get married to anyone."

Jonadab says, "That's good, Amnon doesn't like it; he says his mom is number one queen."

The men change the subject to other things.

Shimeah gets David alone later and says, "I was getting asked that question a lot, so I checked it out. I thought you should know. You should see her, David, proclaiming her spot as number one queen."

The next day, David finds out where the charade happens and sneaks behind a boulder to listen and get a peek.

He hears Amnon objecting, "Stop saying that! My mom is number one!"

Bathsheba has climbed up on top of a boulder, her long black hair blowing in the wind. She doesn't look like a child as she towers over them.

She says, "I am the number one queen!"

Right then, she spots David's head peeking out from below her. She points to him and shouts, "And David, I will love you always!"

David is not laughing. He feels like an arrow shot from her finger to his heart. He is stunned.

… So ends book one.

Study questions:

Why did David have so many wives? For pride?
For security? For alliances? For love?

What is love?

What can you do to guard your own heart?

—ɯɯ—

APPENDIX ONE

Genealogy of King David

Salmon marries Rahab
(harlot from Jericho)

Elimelech marries Naomi
They have two sons. They leave
Bethlehem and move to Moab.
The sons marry in Moab but die
without having children.
Elimelech dies.

One son born

Naomi returns to Bethlehem.

Boaz

One, Daughter-in-law Ruth,
goes with Naomi.

Boaz marries Ruth from Moab

Obed, a son born to them

Obed has a son, Jesse

Jesse, father to eight sons, two daughters.
Jesse's youngest son is
David, who will become the King of Israel.

APPENDIX TWO

David solved problems, and here is one problem some people have about David. I think it can be solved easily.

In the book of I Samuel 17:12, it is said he is the eighth son. I Chronicles 2:17 lists him as the seventh son. The simple answer is that Chronicles is listing genealogy. One of David's older brothers must have died without marrying or having children. He died without any family to record, so he is left out.

Three of David's brothers are mentioned more than once in the Bible: Eliab, Abinadab, and Shammah. They are David's oldest brothers.

The next three brothers, Nethanel, Raddai, and Ozem are only listed in the Chronicles genealogy. My interpretation is that the later three were not as influential in David's life. That is why I have not included them in this story.

APPENDIX THREE

From the encyclopedia for Master Study Bible, ASB, © 1979 Holman Company, Nashville, Tennessee.

Anoint: To apply oil to the head or to other portions of the body—also to things. This was a common and favored custom among the Jews, who had various forms of anointing, depending on the occasion. Ordinary anointing was a customary matter of cleansing. (2 Samuel 12:20, Daniel 10:3, Matt. 6:17). Illustrations: anointing the body (Deut. 28:40, Ruth 3:3, Esther 2:12, Ps. 92:10) anointing of things (Ex. 29:36, 30:26,27 Lev. 8:10,11) ceremonial anointing of persons (Ex. 29:7, 29 Num. 35:25; I Kings 19:16; Is. 61:10).

APPENDIX FOUR

Because he is Jesse's eighth son, other authors have thought David was a boy when he fought Goliath. They are calculating the third oldest, Shammah, is only twenty at that time. And then they allow up to a couple of years between brothers. In their guess, David is depicted as ten to twelve years old.

It is not known in David's family if there are any sets of twins or how long between births. And Shammah could be older than twenty. Shammah is the youngest son listed as a soldier, but that does not mean the next sons were not old enough to be soldiers. Are they even fit for service as soldiers? Do some brothers have other trades?

David's uncle is a wise man who serves as an advisor. Maybe one of David's brothers is a scribe. Maybe some brothers are cooks or work in Saul's fields. So, because Shammah is the youngest listed as soldier, it does not mean he just enlisted at twenty years old.

Saul appoints David to be a captain over soldiers after he kills Goliath. If David is a boy, Saul would certainly not have done that. Therefore, I concluded that when David killed Goliath, he must have been a young man.

APPENDIX FIVE

URIM, THUMMIN (lights, perfections)
Certain objects essential to the act of divination by which in early times the Hebrews sought to learn the will of God. They seem to have opposite meanings, as yes and no, light and darkness. Scholars are not agreed as to the exact meaning of either word (encyclopedia to the Master Study Bible © 1979).

APPENDIX SIX

David brought two wives with him to Hebron. He married four more wives while at Hebron. He was king there seven years and six months. These are the sons born to him at Hebron, listed with each of their mothers.

1. Amnon, son of Ahinoam from Jezreel

2. Chileab or Daniel, son of Abigail, widow of Nabal

3. Absalom, son of Maacah, the daughter of Talmai, the king of Geshur, brother of Tamar

4. Adonijah, son of Haggith

5. Shephatiah, son of Abital

6. Ithream, son of Eglah

APPENDIX SEVEN

I don't know whether David is the one who changed Shammah's name. But in II Samuel, Jonadab and Jonathan are called sons of Shimeah, David's brother. And in I Chronicles 2:13, Jesse's third son is Shimeah, meaning fame. In I Samuel, Jesse's third son was Shammah, meaning destruction.

There are two ways to spell Shimea or Shimeah in English. It is a Hebrew name.

Someone gave him a name change. I think it took a king. I think it had to be someone who knew him well—someone like his brother, David.

END NOTES

In Book I, David has grown from shepherd, to captain, to king. He has many wives and several children. He has been crowned king over Judah. He is only in his thirties and will live to be seventy. There is so much more of his story.

In Book II, David will extend his kingdom. He will be king over all Israel. His wives and children will bring both blessings and trouble. His choices both good and bad will follow him throughout his life. He will be blessed and corrected by God. Even as he dies, he is surrounded by both spies and loved ones.

ABOUT THE AUTHOR

Mary M. Stegmiller was a correspondent for the Quad City Times and the Sterling Gazette for several years. Her principal occupation has been nursing. She worked as an RN for over thirty years and has now retired from correspondence and nursing to become an author, coach, and speaker. This soon-to-be septuagenarian has experienced many *lumps* in her own life. Past experiences include being divorced twice and married three times. She is also a mother, grandmother, and great-grandmother. Because of God's love and intervention, she has been able to *carry on*. In the past, she was reluctant to share her own life experiences, but now she has overcome this. She is a certified coach in the programs that have helped her: *Your Secret Name, The Deeper Path*, and *Day Job to Dream Job.*

She writes, **"I hope my readers will laugh, cry, find courage, and "carry on."**

Alive With the Bible ™

Website: www.alivewiththebible.com

Story and artwork by J.J. Stoecker, shared with permission, not for reproduction.

"I met Jesus in my dreaming once. He was pulling weeds in a garden patch that was completely encircled by fog. I walked up and asked him what I should do with my life. He said, "Feed the people—keep them warm."
After a pause, I said, "Is that it?"
He looked at me and said, "Isn't that enough?"
I've thought about that dream many times."
Here's a logo I did after waking from that:

**Merchandise soon to be available at
www.alivewiththebible.com**

**Discover your secret name—become
the person God created you to be.
Turn your *deepest wound* into the area of
your *biggest impact.***

This course made a huge difference in my life. I was stuck in self-sabotage, depression, and a feeling of worthlessness. It was not until I completed this course and learned my secret name that I could put myself forward enough to write this book.

—Mary Stegmiller

Self-study course available at
https://vy226.isrefer.com/go/ysn5ws/kmsteg21/

There are limited slots available to receive coaching from Mary. Requests can be made for group or individual coaching and/or speaking engagements at:

www.alivewiththebible.com

Stop Living the Unlived Life
Discover Your Purpose
Why are you here?

**A SIMPLE METHOD FOR FINDING
CLARITY, MASTERING LIFE,
AND DOING YOUR PURPOSE EVERYDAY**

Self-study course available at
https://vt226.isrefer.com/go/dpccssw/kmsteg21/

**For more information:
www.alivewiththebible.com**

Is your job a *passion* or a *prison*?
Discover your direction.

Where do you want to go?

Craft your 9-step Dream Job Planner

Self-study course available at:
https://vt226.isref.com/go/djbtcmpss/kmsteg21/

coaching or more information also at

www.alivewiththebible.com

—꿈—

How did I complete writing this book?
Answer-I received help.
More info on becoming an author found at:

https://vt226.isref.com/go/aacad/kmsteg21/

CPSIA information can be obtained
at www.ICGtesting.com
Printed in the USA
FFHW021920241119
56106864-62175FF